MY SISTER'S INTENDED

MY
SISTER'S
INTENDED

RACHAEL
ANDERSON

HEA Publishing

Cover image credit: Ilina Simeonova/Trevillion images

ISBN: 978-1-941363-23-2

Published by HEA Publishing

FOR JEFF
MY CONFIDANTE
MY FRIEND
MY HERO

OTHER BOOKS BY RACHAEL ANDERSON

Regency Novels
The Fall of Lord Drayson (Tanglewood 1)
The Rise of Miss Notley (Tanglewood 2)
The Pursuit of Lady Harriett (Tanglewood 3)

Contemporary Novels
Prejudice Meets Pride (Meet Your Match 1)
Rough Around the Edges Meets Refined (Meet Your Match 2)
Stick in the Mud Meets Spontaneity (Meet Your Match 3)
Not Always Happenstance (Power of the Matchmaker)
The Reluctant Bachelorette
Working it Out
Minor Adjustments
Luck of the Draw
Divinely Designed

Novellas
Righting a Wrong
Twist of Fate
The Meltdown Match

ONE

A SHRILL VOICE grated from across the room. "Prudence Edith Gifford!"

Prudence quickly snapped shut the book she had been reading and tucked it beneath the pillow sitting on her lap. Over the years, she'd learned to discern her mother's mood from the sound her skirts made. A slow and airy swish meant she had nothing to fear, but a hasty scroop, as Prudence heard now, was another matter entirely.

Drat.

Her mother stepped into view wearing her orange taffeta with yellow lace around her pale neck. Combined with her flushed face and blonde curls, she looked very much like the large dahlia growing just outside the study's window. Prudence's father was away from home for a week, and she had thought this room the safest place to read without discovery.

She had been mistaken.

"Good morning, Mother." Prudence managed a bright smile.

In answer, her mother's eyebrows formed a displeased V. Without a word, she snatched the pillow from her daughter's lap and revealed the book Prudence had procured only

1

yesterday. The title, *The Romance of the Forest,* seemed to rise from the cover in an accusing fashion, as though saying, *Yes, this is the nonsense that is sullying the mind of your daughter.*

Prudence scowled at the book until it, too, was snatched from her lap.

"You are supposed to be practicing the pianoforte, not corrupting your mind with this . . . this *rubbish.*"

Prudence nearly blurted, "It is not rubbish," before she had the presence of mind to clamp her mouth shut. Her mother's stern expression would become thunderous indeed if her daughter defended such a book. This was not the first time a conversation of this nature had occurred between them—or probably the last. It was a sorry plight indeed to be born the imaginative daughter of the most unyielding stickler alive.

"Have you nothing to say for yourself?" shrilled her mother's voice again. She shook the book as though it provided the proof needed to convict her daughter of some dastardly deed.

Prudence glanced sorrowfully at the book, knowing it would be the last time she saw that particular copy. Her mother had learned ages ago that she could not return such books to the library or they would eventually find their way back into her daughter's hands. Instead, she would toss it into the fire and require Prudence to pay for its loss with her dwindling pin money. A petition would be made to the proprietress—again—not to lend Miss Prudence Gifford any more novels.

What her mother didn't know, however, was that Mrs. Clampton had not loaned Prudence that book. She had loaned it to Miss Abigail Nash, Prudence's dearest friend, and it was Abby who had passed it along. Unfortunately, her mother would most likely discover Abby's involvement, and that would be the end of that arrangement. She was nothing if not thorough.

Prudence blew a puff of air from the side of her mouth and frowned. After today, she would have to find another co-conspirator, but who? Her sister, Sophia, had attempted to borrow a book for her the previous summer, but she had been found out and had promised never to do so again. Perhaps one of the Calloway twins? Did she dare ask such a thing of them?

Goodness. Ever since her mother had seized control of Prudence's life, things had been a great deal more complicated. How she missed her governess! The woman had not only been a wonderful teacher, but when Prudence had been a young girl and the sun went down and dark shadows, creaks, and imaginings threatened her peace of mind, Miss Simpson would sit beside her and invent story after story. Happy stories, adventurous stories, romantic stories—stories that helped Prudence forget her worries and drift off to sleep.

As she grew older, the fears subsided but her yearning for a good tale did not. When Miss Simpson's services were no longer required and she left the family, Prudence lost both a dear friend and a master storyteller. To ease the sadness, she'd begun to borrow books and create her own stories. It soon became a bit of an obsession.

"Please do not burn it, Mother," she pleaded. "It is Mrs. Clampton's only copy, and she would be greatly saddened to learn of its demise."

"*She* will be greatly saddened?"

Too late, Prudence realized she ought to have at least pretended to be more concerned with her mother's feelings than Mrs. Clampton's. She braced herself for the scolding that would surely come.

3

RACHAEL ANDERSON

"Do you have any idea how saddened *I* am to learn that you have disobeyed my wishes yet again?" It was a question Prudence wisely refrained from answering. "I cannot account for it—or you. Honestly, child, I do not know what to make of you. You embroider the loveliest creations I have ever beheld, you sing like an angel, play beautifully, and you speak nearly flawless French. Once Sophia marries and you make your come out, you have the potential to outshine every other debutante. Yet you continually persist in filling your mind with nonsense. You are a child no longer, Prudence. It is past time to start behaving like the well-bred young lady you are."

She gave *The Romance of the Forest* an angry shake before casting it into the fireplace.

Prudence watched sadly as the dried pages of the book caught flame and slowly shriveled into black, unreadable ash. She shuddered, thinking of all the scribblings she kept hidden beneath a loose floorboard in her room and what would become of them if her mother discovered their existence.

There was a reason Prudence was so interested in reading what her mother called rubbish. More than anything else in the world, the daughter of the distinguished Mr. and Mrs. Gifford wanted to *write* rubbish.

But it wasn't rubbish, not to Prudence.

From the time she was a young girl, scene after scene, story after story, played through her mind like acts on a stage. Imagined characters became people with personalities, interests, motivations, and plights of their own. Prudence couldn't help but get lost to a world more adventurous than her own where anything could happen. She had survived hours embroidering and practicing the pianoforte by shifting her thoughts to this other place. In an instant, she could leave tedium behind and become an innocent maiden who had been trapped in a cellar and forced to do needlepoint at the hand of a villain.

She entered that imaginative world now, envisioning herself as a bullied daughter of a taskmaster, compelled to mold herself into the likeness of a stern mother. If only a handsome rescuer would charge through the door and sweep her away.

Sadly, there would be no rescuer, not today at any rate. Such were the disappointments of reality. Perhaps that was why Prudence loved her imaginary worlds so much. She had the control to shape things according to her wishes. If she wanted a heroine to stand up to her mother, the heroine would. If she wanted a handsome man to enter the room at that precise moment, he would. And if she wanted a book to be saved from the embers, it would have struck the mantle instead of the grate.

Her mother sighed and sat down next to Prudence on the worn brocade sofa, placing her hand over her daughter's in a rare show of affection. "These stories you read are not real, my darling, and I worry about the ideas they are planting in your mind. The more you read, the more discontented you seem with your life. It's as though you're waiting for a dashing man to waltz into town, romance you, and take you on some grand adventure."

Prudence dropped her gaze to her hands, thinking of how many times she *had* wished for that very thing—how many times she had told herself that it *would* happen one day.

The way her mother spoke, however, that day would never come.

Her mother continued. "I had hoped that when your father and I agreed to let you out in society with Sophia this summer that you would set these stories aside, but the opposite has occurred. I now discover you reading more often, you are in a constant state of distraction, and you seem disinterested in most of the people you meet."

Prudence bit her lower lip, knowing her mother spoke the truth—or at least a portion of the truth. "I am not disinterested," she said. "I adore Sophia and Abby and think the Calloway twins are most diverting."

"Sophia is your sister and Abby your dearest friend. Of course you adore them. And the only reason you find the twins so diverting is because they behave like children."

Prudence had to concede the truth of that as well, but why did it matter? "I don't understand why you are so troubled, Mother. When you allowed me out into society, you made it clear that I should blend into the background and not be on the hunt for a husband just yet. Sophia needs to marry first, as we both know, so why does it bother you that I find most people—especially the men—somewhat tiresome? Shouldn't that be a good thing?"

"For now, yes," agreed her mother. "I only worry that you will have the same attitude when you make your bows. You cannot expect to marry a man like one of those heroes from your silly books. Yes, I have read one or two of them and found them ridiculous in the extreme."

Prudence frowned, not appreciating her mother's perspective. Was it so wrong to want to marry a man who was handsome, intelligent, witty, kind, and charming? Her mother made it sound as though that combination did not exist. But surely it did.

Surely.

"Once we go to London," said Prudence. "I'm certain there will be at least a few men among the ton who will not disappoint."

"And if you should meet such a man?" her mother persisted. "Do you believe he will want to marry a woman who is often distracted and places greater importance on reading silly books than taking her duties as wife, mother, and mistress of a household seriously?"

Prudence swallowed and shifted uncomfortably. Her mother had never spoken this plainly before. She had only blustered and commanded and tossed books into fires. But now that her words were hovering over her, Prudence had to wonder if they had merit. Was she too easily distracted? Had she formed unrealistic expectations of what her life should be? Had she grown tired of reality and preferred to live in her imaginary worlds?

Perhaps in a way, she realized with dismay.

But how could she give up her dreams and aspirations of becoming published one day? It was so much a part of her that . . . no, she couldn't. Nor should she have to. Ann Radcliffe hadn't given it up. Neither had Fanny Burney, Charlotte Lennox, Samuel Richardson, Walter Scott, Henry Fielding, or Maria Edgeworth.

Prudence's brow furrowed as she considered Miss Edgeworth and the fact that she had never married. Why hadn't she? Did she prefer a life surrounded by books with no one telling her what to do? Or perhaps the woman hadn't been able to settle for a life outside her own imaginings. Had she wanted to become a wife and a mother but had never found a man she felt was worthy of her—as Prudence's mother accused her of doing? Was Prudence destined to follow a similar path?

No. She would never allow that to happen. Although she had dreams of becoming a novelist, she also wanted to be a wife, a mother, a contributor to society. She wanted to have it all and believed she *could* have it all.

But perhaps her mother was right about one thing. Perhaps she was too easily distracted and needed to lower her expectations somewhat. Prudence could certainly try a little harder in those areas.

"I can see your point, Mother," she finally said. "But you cannot ask me to give up reading altogether. I could never do it. Would you consider a compromise instead?"

The V shape in her mother's eyebrows returned, along with pinched lips. She probably didn't think agreements should be made between mothers and daughters, but she didn't immediately dismiss the request either, which gave Prudence some hope.

"If you will allow me to borrow one book every month, I promise to limit my reading to that one book alone. I shall also make an increased effort at being more . . . aware." That was a fair compromise, was it not?

Her mother nodded slowly, as though considering the proposal. Prudence waited anxiously, wondering if there would ever be a day when they could claim an understanding of one another. They had always been so different, both in personalities and looks. Where her mother was tall, sturdy, fair, and excessively proper, Prudence was petite, slender, dark-haired, and decidedly *im*proper. She always thought that she should have been given the name Sophia and Sophia, Prudence. They would have fit a great deal better.

If only Prudence's mother would at least *attempt* to understand her younger daughter.

At long last her mother gave a curt nod. "Very well. But *I* shall be the one to accompany you to the library and aid you with the selection of your books."

Prudence frowned, not liking that stipulation at all. It wasn't much of a compromise if it could be considered one at all. She opened her mouth to say as much, but her mother had already clapped her hands together as though they had reached a satisfying agreement.

"Now that we have settled that, I would like you to fetch your gloves and boots and accompany Sophia to the dress-maker's. As you know, we have accepted the invitation for Mr. and Mrs. Hilliard's dance on Friday next, and I have decided to splurge a little, just this once."

"New gowns for a small country dance?" Prudence asked, thinking it rather odd. Her mother had always been of an economical nature, never condoning the purchase of a new gown for such an unexceptional event.

"I have learned, only this morning, that Lord Knave is returning to Radbourne Abbey and will most likely be in attendance. Therefore, I would like Sophia to appear to her greatest advantage. You have quite the eye for fashion, my dear, and I would appreciate your assistance in choosing a gown for her. Nothing extravagant, of course—no added lace or embroidery—merely something that will set her apart from the others. Now that she is close to making her bows, I'm certain Lord Knave will wish to further his acquaintance with her."

Ah, so it is only Sophia who will receive a new gown, thought Prudence wryly. She should have realized as much, not that she cared. After the harrowing months her sister had endured this past year, she deserved a new dress and any other good thing life had to offer. Prudence would never begrudge Sophia anything. She was alive and well, and that's all that mattered.

Prudence *did* care about the loss of her books, however, and wondered if she needed to uphold the so-called "com-promise" she had made with her mother. It had been more of a decree than an agreement, after all, so she shouldn't be *required* to comply. She certainly hadn't promised to do so.

At the same time, if her mother were to ever catch Prudence reading an unapproved book, she would be accused of going back on her word. That did not sit well with her. Over the years, Prudence had often defied her mother's wishes, but she had never broken anything resembling a promise and had no wish to do so now.

Blast.

How would she continue to write without her only source of useful information—books? Prudence could never write what she did not know, and at this point in her life, most of her knowledge about love and romance came from the words and experiences of others. She needed to continue reading if she was to continue writing, and if she adhered to her mother's wishes, she couldn't do either.

Oh, what a conundrum.

"I do hope you will stay out of Sophia's way at the dance and attempt to blend in more than you usually do," said her mother with a worried look. "It will be an important night for her, and . . . well, your time will come in another year, my pet, as soon as we have Sophia wedded to Lord Knave."

Prudence stared at her mother in confusion. Stay out of Sophia's way? Blend in more than she usually did? What on earth had she meant by that? It almost sounded as though she wished her younger daughter were invisible.

"If you'd rather I not go to the dance, Mother, I am perfectly content to remain at home." On a hopeful note, she quickly added, "Especially if you allow me to borrow a book of my choosing from the lending library."

Her mother's jaw tightened, showing her displeasure at the suggestion. "We have already sent our acceptance, so we will *all* be going regardless of whether you want to or not, and we only just agreed that *I* will be choosing the books you lend."

"Actually, we did not—"

"Now off you go," her mother said dismissively. "The gowns need to be ordered today if they are to be ready in time."

Prudence fumed as she left the room. Her mother wouldn't even try to understand. She thought she knew what was best for her daughter, but she didn't. How could she when they were nothing alike?

Prudence suddenly pictured herself as a puppet. If her mother wanted her to dance, she would dance. If her mother wanted her to perform on the pianoforte, she'd perform. If her mother wanted her to sing, she would sing. And if her mother wanted her to cease reading novels, she would be expected to comply. Because that's what puppets did. They submitted to the ones who held the strings.

Someday, Prudence would find a way to break free from the constraints, but until that day came, she would not be completely manipulated. Perhaps she could persuade Mrs. Clampton to switch the covers on a few books? Probably not. Or maybe Mrs. Hilliard had some novels tucked away in her library somewhere? Yes, that could work. Quite nicely, in fact.

Prudence would do as her mother bid. She would help her sister choose a new gown and see to it that Sophia was the most radiant woman at the dance. With all eyes on her, no one would see the younger Gifford daughter slip away to the library.

What better way to "blend in" after all?

TWO

THE AFTERNOON WAS warm and glorious with skies free of clouds and air free of everything but a delightful breeze. South Oxfordshire didn't get too many afternoons such as these, even in the summer, so Prudence had learned to appreciate them whenever they came along.

She and her sister had begged to walk to town, and their mother had eventually relented so long as they took their maid with them. Ruth now trailed behind, giving the girls some privacy—not that they needed it. Ever since Sophia had succumbed to an illness the previous year, she had withdrawn and never seemed to have much to say anymore. Prudence hadn't minded because it gave her more time to contemplate her stories, but as she glanced at her sister now, she realized how far apart they'd grown and how she missed the friendship they once shared.

Sophia was no longer sickly. Perhaps it was time to stop treating her as such.

As they strolled along the road, a striking sandstone house came into view, and not for the first time Prudence contemplated the structure. A combination of Palladian and Baroque styles, Radbourne Abbey stood out against the rolling green hills like a queen among commoners. The columns spanning the front commanded attention, and the

13

array of windows made Prudence want to peek inside. She had never been afforded the opportunity, but she imagined marble floors, gleaming wood, and expansive rooms.

The house had served as inspiration for the hero's home in a story she had begun writing at the beginning of the summer—*The Troubles of Counte Montague*. The scene she was currently working on involved a heated discussion between the hero and his parents. He wanted to close up half the house and his parents wouldn't hear of it. They insisted that he—

No, she would not think of that story now. She had determined to let it rest for the afternoon, and that is precisely what she intended to do. Prudence glanced at her sister then at Radbourne Abbey once more, wondering about its occupants. She did not know Lord and Lady Bradden well, but when the time came for them to officially announce the betrothal of their son, The Viscount Knave, to Miss Sophia Gifford, that would undoubtedly change.

"How well acquainted are you with Lord Knave?" Prudence asked.

Sophia appeared momentarily surprised by the broken silence. She quickly recovered and followed Prudence's gaze, squinting in the direction of the house. "As well as you, I imagine."

"I do not know him at all," said Prudence. "I have seen him in the distance, waved at him a time or two, but whenever Mother invited him and Lord and Lady Bradden to dine at Talford, I was always sent to the schoolroom. Thus, I have never made his acquaintance."

"No, I suppose you haven't had the chance, have you?" Under the brim of her wide linen bonnet, Sophia appeared troubled. "It is not right, or fair, that your come out has been delayed on account of my illness. I am sorry for it."

"'Tis nothing." Prudence waved her sister's concern aside. If everything had gone according to plan, Sophia would already be married to Lord Knave and Prudence would be preparing for her own London season. Unfortunately, rheumatic fever had kept Sophia homebound for nearly nine months and on the brink of death for part of that time.

How difficult those months had been. Her parents had tried to send Prudence away to her aunt's, but she had begged to remain, saying she could never pretend as though nothing was amiss when everything was. It had taken a great deal of convincing, but they relented at last, making Prudence promise to stay far away from the sickroom.

She had kept her promise, keeping to her bedchamber, the parlor, the library, and taking long walks when the weather permitted. But the sickness had gone on and on, taking a turn for the worse one day and a turn for the better the next. The months of perpetual concern, endless quiet, and loneliness caused Prudence to escape to her stories with more zeal than ever. They—and her visits to her friend Abby—became her only source of relief from the fear of losing her sister.

Prudence had prayed, she had cried, she had started a story about two sisters who had been as close as close could be until smallpox stole the life of one of them. Why Prudence had allowed the story to veer in that direction, she didn't know. She only knew that it had caused her to shed a great many tears and feel miserable—at least until she'd tossed the last half of the story into the fire and rewritten the ending to something much happier.

Thankfully, it was her revised outcome that had come to fruition. Sophia had fully recovered and now walked at Prudence's side free from any of the lasting struggles that affected many rheumatic fever sufferers. Her heart remained strong and her joints were free from pain.

"I begged Mother to allow both of us to be presented at court, but she wouldn't consider it," said Sophia. "She said it is not the thing, but in truth, I think she worries that you would capture all of the attention. Where would that leave me if Lord Knave does not come up to scratch? I would become the spinster sister of the most sought-after debutante in England." Sophia smiled to show that she was teasing, but her expression contained an element of truth.

Prudence's heart ached at the sight. It was true that her sister's red hair and freckles were far from fashionable and she wasn't quite as accomplished as her younger sister, but Sophia was beautiful and talented and more of a lady than Prudence would ever be. If her sister lacked for anything, it was confidence.

"A man would have to be bacon-brained not to notice you," said Prudence firmly.

Sophia laughed. "Not if you are standing next to me. He wouldn't be able to help himself, and rightly so. You are gorgeous in the fashionable sense and have an air of confidence about you that cannot be overlooked."

"Nonsense, Sophia," said Prudence. "It wouldn't take more than a moment or two for a man to realize that you are the gem and I am nothing more than a silly bluestocking. And if Mother truly believes me capable of stealing your suitors, which are sure to be in great supply, she would have kept me homebound this summer instead of allowing me out into local society. I most certainly would not have her permission to attend Mrs. Hilliard's dance next week, especially when Lord Knave is likely to attend—not that any of this matters as you are practically betrothed to the man."

"Oh, I wouldn't say that," said Sophia. "One day I hope to be betrothed to him, but it is not a guarantee."

That was news to Prudence. For as long as she could remember, *When Sophia weds Lord Knave* . . . had been a frequent topic of conversation. Why would her parents speak of their union as though it was a certainty if it wasn't? They wouldn't. Sophia was simply being her usual unassuming self.

"I'm sure he is merely waiting for you to make your bows before asking for your hand," said Prudence.

"That is what both of our parents are hoping for, what *I* am hoping for, but he is under no obligation to do so and has never implied as much to me. Honestly, I do not know what his plans are with regard to me."

Prudence frowned at her sister. "He has never implied anything of the sort? Are you sure? What *have* you spoken to him about?"

Sophia's forehead wrinkled in thought before she shrugged. "I can't say for certain. I fell ill before we had too many opportunities to get to know one another. When we dined together, our parents were present, and I don't believe I contributed much to the conversation. And the few times we danced together, I can only recall discussing the weather or the graciousness of our host and hostess. Nothing of consequence."

The weather? The graciousness of their hosts? Prudence could scarce believe it. She had always assumed the two had known each other as children, at least a little, and had maintained some level of correspondence over the years. They were to be married, after all.

"Were you not playmates when you were younger?" she asked.

"No."

"Have you never bumped into him while out riding?" Sophia adored riding. Aside from the months she spent in the sickroom, she could be found racing across the meadows on any clear day. Surely they had encountered each other at some point.

"Only from a distance, but I never approached him, nor did he approach me."

Prudence stopped walking and took her sister by the arm, causing her to stop as well. "Do you mean to tell me that you are planning to marry a man you hardly know?"

She nodded as though it was nothing out of the ordinary.

"Why the devil would you agree to such a thing?"

Sophia appeared startled by her sister's vehemence, but she did not chide her for it. Instead, she offered up an explanation that sounded more rehearsed than anything else. "Lord Knave will one day be the Earl of Bradden and the master of Radbourne Abbey, as well as a number of other, smaller estates."

Prudence waited for her to continue, and when she did not, she prodded, "And . . .?"

Sophia rolled her eyes as though her reasons should be obvious. "And if I marry him, I will become a wealthy countess. In return, he will be marrying the heiress to Talford Hall. Once I come into my inheritance and the two estates are joined, we will be the largest landowners in the county."

Prudence's eyes widened in astonishment. All these years, talk of marriage between the two families had been nothing more than a business arrangement? What if they did not care for one another? What if he turned out to be a tyrant or a rake or a bounder? What if he was the sort of man her sister could never grow to love or even care for?

"You cannot be serious," Prudence whispered.

"But I am. Why else would I marry if not for the enticement that I will one day be a countess?"

Prudence had no words for this. She could only gawk at her sister in what was surely a most unladylike fashion. "What if you cannot love him?" she squeaked.

Sophia smiled a little and shook her head, making Prudence feel as though she was back in the schoolroom, being laughed at for her fanciful notions.

"I'm fairly certain I can find *something* to love in him, even if it is only his house, his title, his wealth, and his person. He is quite handsome, you know."

Prudence was not appeased. Perhaps she had read too many novels or invented too many stories, but she desperately wanted to feel the euphoria of falling in love—the sort of love that made titles and wealth and mansions inconsequential, not that Prudence would complain if the man she fell in love with had those things. But she didn't require them. She only required a man who could make her heart leap, her skin tingle, and her world ignite with endless possibilities.

How could her sister consider settling for less?

"You think me unromantic, don't you?" asked Sophia.

Prudence couldn't even pretend she didn't think it. "Unromantic, without passion, and mad."

Sophia laughed. "Let us see how mad I am when I am mistress of Radbourne Abbey and wife to a handsome earl. You, on the other hand, are welcome to marry Mr. Winston, with his small cottage and only one servant. But you will love him dearly, so none of that will matter, will it?"

Prudence grimaced at the very idea of being saddled to that man. "I could never love Mr. Winston. He is far too serious."

"'Tis a pity you think that," said Sophia with a grin. "I think he fancies himself in love with you."

"What rot," said Prudence, even though she, too, had noticed an increase in his attentions of late, especially at the last dance she'd attended at the town hall. He had attempted to claim her hand for three dances, instead of the acceptable two, and she had been forced to feign dizziness and ask that he procure her a glass of lemonade instead. He stubbornly remained at her side through two additional dances until she had spied her friend across the room and said, "Poor Miss Nash is without a partner. Do say you will be her rescuer, sir."

Mr. Winston had jumped up to do her bidding, and Prudence had sent her friend an apologetic glance before seeking out her mother and claiming a headache. They had left the dance early that night, and it was all because of the dratted Mr. Winston. She could only pray he had not been invited to Mrs. Hilliard's dance.

It was a fledgling hope, but she clung to it nonetheless.

Not wanting to discuss Mr. Winston further, Prudence said, "Should I ever fall in love with a man who has only a small cottage and one servant, I would be more content married to him than to a man of fortune who I could never love."

"Would you continue to love him, I wonder, when you are required to help with the washing, cooking, and mending? How romantic would life be then?"

Not at all romantic, Prudence thought, realizing she had probably spoken with a little too much conviction. "I will simply have to fall in love with a man of means."

Sophia laughed. "So we are able to select the men we fall in love with now, is that it? In that case, I choose to fall in love with Lord Knave."

Prudence shook her head and smiled, understanding her sister and not understanding her at the same time. Yes, it sounded wonderful to live in Radbourne Abbey as the wife of a handsome and wealthy earl, but if they could not come to love, admire, or even like each other, that large house would feel more empty than luxurious, wouldn't it?

Was it so wrong to want to love and be loved? Was it wrong to want to read about love and write about love and experience love? And if it *was* so wrong, or merely a ridiculous fantasy, why did Prudence desire it so very much?

THREE

DURING THE CARRIAGE ride to the Hilliards, Prudence didn't even attempt conversation. She was far too glum. As the carriage jostled her family along, she thought back over her many frustrations of the past week. Each night she had listened until all household sounds had died down before lifting the floorboard near the edge of her bed, removing the stack of foolscap, and crawling back into bed with her pencil in hand and a small candle flickering at her side.

Then she'd waited.

And waited.

And waited.

For nothing.

No interesting conversations emerged, no scenes played out in her mind, and no new characters surfaced. Instead, her existing characters seemed to lose any and all motivations. They became lifeless and droll and so very vexing.

Prudence had at last tossed the papers aside, blaming her mother for taking away her one and only source of inspiration. Whenever she would read, her mind would come alive with dialogue, strategies, and interesting twists and turns. Sometimes she'd dismiss them as ridiculous and other times she would write furiously. Regardless, the ideas would come. They'd always come.

Until now.

"Here we are." Her mother's voice broke into her thoughts, and Prudence realized they had arrived at the Hilliards.

She glanced out of the window at the inviting house before her. A wide staircase led up to a charming red brick house with a dozen windows blinking candlelight. It was a romantic site to behold, with beautifully dressed ladies ascending the steps on the arms of well-dressed men, but Prudence couldn't make herself feel enthused. She had planned to sneak away to the library for the evening, and had thought it a grand idea for a time, but as she worked over the logistics, she came to the aggravating conclusion that her mother would eventually notice her absence and come looking for her. She would have time to read a chapter or two, but that was all, and who wanted to begin a story they could not finish?

Not her. So once again, she was subject to the controlling strings of her mother.

Prudence climbed from the carriage with a sigh, knowing that nothing fresh or different would happen on the other side of those walls. The ballroom was bound to be unbearably stuffy, the drinks lukewarm, and Mr. Winston was probably lying in wait, ready to pounce and claim her first two, possibly three, dances. Not even Lord Knave's impending arrival sparked an interest in her. From Sophia's descriptions, he sounded as though he would get along with Mr. Winston all too well.

Prudence should have pled a headache and not come at all, not that her mother would have countenanced such a thing.

Just as she feared, the moment they were shown into the ballroom, Mr. Winston solicited her hand for the first dance.

She nodded and mustered a kind smile while mentally preparing herself for what would undoubtedly be the longest evening of her life. Surely London would be more exciting than this. It had to be.

"Miss Prudence, you'll never guess what I discovered in my wheat fields this morning. A turnip plant. Can you imagine?"

Yes, Prudence could imagine it, especially considering the man had harvested turnips from the same field the previous fall. He'd given her a detailed history of his crop rotations the last time they'd spoken. She feigned an interest and muttered a few intelligible responses, knowing he did not want—or expect—an actual discussion.

She proceeded to listen with only half an ear as the music played on and on and on, wishing she could think of some adventurous tale to help whittle away the time, but all her mind conjured up was the image of a servant girl weeding turnips from the wheat.

Insipid, colorless, unimaginative.

When at last the dance concluded, Mr. Winston tucked her hand into the crook of his elbow and led her back in the direction of her mother. "You are looking well tonight, Miss Prudence. That gown is the color of my wheat field in the early-morning light. Do say you will honor me with the supper dance."

Prudence attempted to hide her dismay. *The supper dance?* Could this man not see they would never suit? Perhaps he would if he took the time to discover her interests, but he spoke only of his plants and the health of his livestock, and while Prudence was not opposed to discussing such matters, he never asked for her opinion. He merely informed while she listened and nodded and said, "I see." If she attempted to steer the conversation in another direction with a comment about politics or books or the latest *on dits*, he would steer it back to his farm.

And now he wanted to continue informing her during the supper dance. What more could he possibly have to say on the subject? She did not wish to find out.

Before she could bring herself to give him an answer, her friend, Miss Abigail Nash, clutched her free arm. "Forgive me, Mr. Winston, but there is a matter of great urgency that I must discuss with my friend."

"There's nothing to forgive," said Mr. Winston gallantly, bowing over Prudence's glove before taking his leave.

Prudence offered her friend a grateful smile. Tall and beautiful, with golden locks and a willowy figure, Abby had never looked more angelic. "What a dear you are, Abby, though I don't deserve it after the way I foisted him on you at the last dance."

"If you think I did that for you, you are mistaken," said Abby. "I was merely looking out for my own interests. Admit it, you were about to suggest that he seek me out so that you might be rid of him."

Prudence shook her head. "I would never do that to you again. In truth, I was about to suggest he take Miss Stevenson into supper instead of me. Don't you think they would make a fine pair? She dislikes speaking, and he adores it."

"Yes, but does she enjoy listening to discourses on the latest plowing methods?" Abby asked.

"I can't say for certain as I have never been able to get her to speak more than a word or two. Have you had better luck?"

"No. She appears so nervous in every situation. I have attempted to converse with her once or twice, thinking I was doing her a kindness, but I don't think she considered it as such. I believe she prefers to be left alone."

Prudence eyed the girl for a moment, wondering if that was the case. Would anyone wish to remain forgotten in the corner, with no dance partners or friends to help pass the hours? Perhaps Prudence should make more of an effort to get to know her. At the very least, she ought to find out whether or not Miss Stevenson had an interest in farming and livestock.

"Did your father come with you tonight?" Prudence asked, casting a quick glance around the ballroom.

"Sadly, no. He is away on one of his business trips again. Great-aunt Josephine accompanied me."

"Oh. Where is she now?"

"At one of the card tables, no doubt." Abby leaned in close and lowered her voice. "Don't look now, but Mr. Winston will not cease glancing your way. I believe he is waiting to swoop in the moment it appears as though our urgent conversation has come to an end."

"For pity's sake." Prudence waved her fan to cool her rising ire. She had no desire to be unkind to anyone as benign as Mr. Winston, but if he did not cease his increased attentions soon, she would have no choice in the matter.

"Is it too much to ask that a charming, interesting, and handsome man enter the room at this very moment, set his sights on me, and shoo away every other man?" asked Prudence. "Does no such a person exist in South Oxford-shire?"

Abby patted her arm kindly. "You will probably have to wait until London to encounter him, unless you plan to steal Lord Knave from your sister." She wiggled her eyebrows and grinned. "I hear he's quite dashing."

Prudence refrained from telling her friend that Lord Knave no more fit her requirements of a dashing gentleman than Mr. Winston did, not that she could fault Abby for placing him in that category. From the moment Prudence arrived, Lord Knave had been on the tip of everyone's tongue. She was certain the entire town had come this evening with the hope of seeing him.

"I hear he will be coming tonight," said Abby, glancing slyly at the entrance.

"That is what my mother and sister are hoping for," said Prudence, examining her gloves.

"But not you?"

Prudence sighed, not wishing to discuss Lord Knave any longer. She kept picturing her sweet sister walking the expansive halls of Radbourne, alone and forlorn while her husband went off to London. "I do not care whether he comes or not. The way everyone speaks his name, with hushed tones and barely suppressed excitement, one would think the Prince Regent himself is coming."

Abby tried to suppress her smile. "If he was promised to you and not your sister, would you care then?"

"I would never be foolish enough to promise myself to any man I did not know or love."

"Of course not," said Abby. "Ever the romantic."

There it was again, that amused tone her sister so often used when Prudence brought up the subject of romance. She was coming to despise the way it pestered her to let go of her dreams.

Never, she thought. *I would rather live out the remainder of my days alone than be subject to a man I do not desire.* Not that Prudence wished for that outcome either.

"Is being a romantic so very wrong?" Prudence asked, more to herself than her friend.

"Not really," said Abby. "One day I very much hope to find a man who will make my heart trill, but I have no expectations to encounter him this evening."

A hush fell over the room, pulling the girls' attention away from the conversation at hand and directing it towards the entrance of the ballroom, not too far from where they stood. A man had paused on the threshold, and Prudence couldn't help but stare. He appeared precisely the way she had pictured Mr. Camden in the book she was currently writing. Tall, distinguished, handsome, and impeccably dressed, he had thick and wavy chestnut hair, piercing blue eyes, and a strong but slightly crooked nose. Confidence seemed to seep from his soul, and Prudence wondered if he was also clever, interesting, and kind.

His gaze swept over the room, pausing for a moment at the far side. A hint of a smile stretched his lips for the merest of seconds before he continued on. Most people probably didn't notice the pause, but Prudence did. She always noticed.

She followed his gaze to find the lovely Mrs. Harper, with her flashing green eyes, silky auburn hair, and well-endowed figure. The poor woman had lost her husband to an accident last summer and had only recently come out of mourning. Her sapphire silk gown attested to it. But as Prudence observed her knowing smile—one that welcomed whatever attention the man on the threshold planned to give her—she no longer felt sorry for Mrs. Harper.

Prudence looked back at the man, watching him closely as his eyes continued to scan the room. They rested briefly on her and Abby, but not for long. In the end, they settled on Sophia. With an expression that could only be described as resolute, he moved forward, greeting his host and hostess, exchanging a few words with some others, and nodding politely at Prudence and Abby as he passed. A moment later, he stopped in front of her sister and their mother and bowed over Sophia's hand. Both women beamed with pride.

So *that* was the infamous Lord Knave. Prudence ought to have known, she supposed, but she had been certain he would not be nearly as handsome as everyone seemed to think.

She had been wrong.

Her sister uttered a few words to him and Lord Knave reciprocated in kind. Her mother inserted a few more, but Sophia and Lord Knave's expressions remained impassive and their smiles artificial. Conversation appeared to be more of a chore than a pleasure for both of them.

A new set began forming, and Lord Knave held out his arm to her sister. As they made their way onto the dance floor, Abby leaned in and whispered, "Don't they look wonderful together?"

Prudence pursed her lips in thought. Oh, they both *looked* handsome—Lord Knave in his dark, tailored jacket and her sister in her new, shimmering green gown. The moment Prudence had spotted that fabric, she had known it was meant for her sister. Not only did it complement her red hair like no other color did, the fabric molded to her sister's curves. Sophia had never looked lovelier. But together, they did not look wonderful. They looked ill at ease.

Is this how they wished to spend the rest of their lives? All for the sake of land and titles?

It was a depressing thought and one Prudence refused to dwell on for long. Perhaps once they came to know each other better, their smiles would become real and the wretched man would cease sneaking glances at the enticing Mrs. Harper when her sister's attention was focused elsewhere. Apparently the respected Lord Knave was not as respectable as he would like people to think. When he and Mrs. Harper exchanged yet another secret look, Prudence's opinion of him plummeted. How could she possibly have compared him to the hero from her book? Mr. Camden was every inch a gentleman, and Lord Knave—well, it seemed his title fit him altogether too well. He was every inch a knave.

A knave who will one day become your brother-in-law, she reminded herself.

"Miss Nash, do say you will dance with me," intruded a welcome voice. It was one of the Calloway twins, come to steal her friend away.

Prudence might have minded, but where there was one twin, the other was never far behind. Ah, here he came now.

He side-stepped around a few people, slid between a few others, and finally arrived at Prudence's side slightly out of breath. "Miss Prudence, I do apologize for arriving in such a state, but I'm afraid it could not be helped. Mrs. Hilliard detained me, allowing my brother an unfair lead."

Prudence looked from one Calloway twin to the other, trying to determine which was which. The brothers were as identical as two twins could be. Their noses were the same narrow shape, their eyes the same shade of gray, and their complexions free from any and all distinguishable blemishes. They even dressed similarly and styled their dark-blond hair alike—swept up on top and brushed forward on the sides. Try as she might, Prudence had never been able to tell them apart, which was exactly what they wanted. The two men— or rather, *boys*—took great delight in baffling those they encountered.

Although Prudence could never take them seriously, she enjoyed their liveliness and humor. They were, by far, her favorite dancing partners.

"Never apologize for arriving out of breath, sir," said Prudence. "It is a compliment to have a man race to one's side."

He leaned in and raised his hand to the side of his face

to keep his words from being overheard. "You should consider it a great compliment then. I spied Freddy Standish coming your way and had to virtually gallop to beat him here."

From the corner of her eye, Prudence spied Freddy not far away, speaking to another young woman. She lowered her voice. "Bless you for your haste. Freddy *always* steps on my toes."

The twin's eyes widened dramatically. "No."

She nodded sadly. "I'm afraid so. He has ruined many a slipper."

"Mine too," added Abby. "I have learned not to wear my best ones to a dance where he is likely to attend."

"Pray tell us that we have never ruined any of your slippers," said the other twin.

"Thankfully, no," said Prudence. "You are both far too graceful to ever do such a thing."

"You relieve our minds greatly," said the twin nearest to Prudence. He took up her hand and bowed over it. "Only tell me that you trust me enough to put your lovely slippers under my protection for the duration of the next dance?"

"That all depends on who is asking, sir."

He feigned an injured look. "Why, Felix, obviously. Do you not recognize me?"

"Actually I do, *Lionel*," she answered, as though she knew without a doubt to which twin she addressed. "I was merely testing your integrity, sir, which I now find lacking. Perhaps I should not dance with you after all."

"Ah, perceptive as usual." He played along as he always did whenever Prudence claimed to know which was which. "What gave me away?"

"The state of your cravat, if you must know. It appears as though you attempted to tie it yourself, which I know Felix would never do."

The one she referred to as Felix barked out a laugh. "I do believe you are right, Miss Prudence. That knot does indeed look pitiful. It couldn't possibly be the work of our valet."

"Not to worry, Lionel," said Abby, reaching over to straighten his neckcloth. "I fix my father's often, so I know precisely what to do. There." She patted his chest. "Good as new."

"Thank you, Abigail. I am in your debt." Lionel shot her a grateful look before returning his attention to Prudence. "I beg you will set your displeasure of me aside for the duration of one dance. Do you think you can? I did gallop to your side, after all."

She managed to keep a straight face while she tapped her lower lip in thought. At last she said, "I suppose I can, but only if you'll agree to gallop to my side again for the supper dance."

"That sounds more like a reward than a penalty," he said gallantly as he led her onto the dance floor. "Perhaps I should fabricate more often."

"I'm not sure you can more often than you already do."

He laughed as the music for the cotillion began. They bowed and curtsied to each other, and when they rose, she joined hands with him and the man on her right to form a large circle.

There was a reason Prudence loved to dance with either of the Callaway twins. They were always cheerful and interesting, quick to smile and laugh, and they never failed to lighten her mood.

But alas, neither had ever made her heart beat in time with her feet.

"Now really, which twin are you?" she asked as they began the set.

"Are you doubting your observational skills?"

"When it comes to you and your brother, I always doubt them."

He chuckled. "Rest assured you have guessed correctly then. I am Lionel."

She studied him from the corner of her eye—the slight tug of his lips, the glow in his eyes, and the merriment in his expression. Prudence might not be able to tell them apart, but she *could* tell when someone was attempting not to laugh at her.

"Drat," she muttered. "You are Felix after all."

He laughed louder this time, drawing the attention of the other dancers. She paid them little mind as she glared at her partner. "Someday, I hope you encounter twin sisters who are every bit as identical and aggravating as you and your brother."

He grinned and leaned in close. "And someday I will tell you the one feature that distinguishes me from my brother, but only because I like you so very much."

She had to smile at that. "I shall hold you to that, sir, but I will not hold my breath that I will discover your secret anytime soon. You like to tease me far too much."

"'Tis true," he said. "Perhaps I shall direct my barrister to send you a letter upon my demise."

She laughed. "Now that, I can believe."

They continued to tease and smile and laugh throughout the remainder of the dance. Upon its conclusion, Felix led Prudence to her mother's side. After a brief exchange, he excused himself to fetch them a drink, promising to return momentarily. Prudence watched him leave, feeling much more cheerful. Not only had he bolstered her spirits but there was now a high probability Felix would save her from an interminable supper with Mr. Winston.

Her mother leaned in close and whispered, "Must you always steal the attention away from your sister?"

Prudence looked at her mother in surprise. "What do you mean?"

"The way you made that boy laugh over and over and over again. It caused quite the scene. Everyone in the entire room was staring, my dear, including your *sister's partner.*" She emphasized the last part as though Prudence was to blame for the man's wandering eyes—eyes which she was sure had never settled on her. He had probably been examining the lovely Mrs. Harper, who had also joined the set.

"The Callaway twins laugh no matter their partner," said Prudence, attempting to keep the exasperation from her tone.

"If you believe that, you are a simpleton indeed."

Feminine laughter came from somewhere nearby, and Prudence was quick to nod in that direction. "See? There is Felix now, making Abby laugh."

"Yes, but is she making *him* laugh?"

"She makes both twins laugh often, Mother. But I fail to see what that has to do with anything. Should no one be allowed to laugh at a dance?" Prudence's voice rose slightly at the injustice of it all. To be accused of stealing away Lord Knave's attention—a man she had no interest in at all. What fustian! She had done nothing to deserve her mother censure. She hadn't even purchased a new gown for tonight's event. All she'd done was allow herself to have a good time with a friend.

"Mother, I—"

"Hush. Here they come." Her mother pasted a welcoming smile on her face while Prudence tried her best not to simmer. "Ah, here you are. Lord Knave, how good of you to return my daughter to me. I do hope you enjoyed the dance."

He nodded and bowed as any proper gentleman would. "Miss Gifford was a delight as always."

Sophia blushed, and their mother's smile widened. "Yes, my lord. She certainly is *always* a delight."

As opposed to your younger daughter, Prudence thought in annoyance.

"Please," said Sophia. "You will bring me to the blush if you do not cease such compliments."

You are already blushing, Prudence thought uncharitably. Did her mother and sister realize they were practically fawning over the man? For what purpose? Her sister would be better served looking elsewhere for a husband.

Prudence didn't fail to notice that her mother had neglected to introduce her to the viscount—not that she wished for an introduction—but it was never a pleasurable experience to be so obviously overlooked.

"Lord Knave," said Sophia, apparently realizing her mother's lapse. "Have you had the pleasure of meeting my sister, Miss Prudence?"

"I don't believe so." He captured Prudence's gaze with a look of open curiosity.

"Forgive me, my lord," their mother rushed to say. "I forget that you are not yet acquainted with my *younger* daughter." She emphasized "younger" as though Prudence was only ten instead of eighteen. Sophia, at nineteen, was apparently a great deal more sophisticated.

Prudence refrained from rolling her eyes at her mother and curtsied instead. "'Tis a pleasure, my lord." She said nothing more even though she wanted to ask him why his gaze continually strayed to Mrs. Harper. Once he married Sophia, would it continue to stray in that woman's direction?

If so, perhaps he ought to marry Mrs. Harper and not her sister.

"Are you planning to make your bows with your sister this season?" he asked.

Prudence glanced at her mother, knowing she would be reprimanded again if she did not play the part of a diminutive younger sister. She probably should have ducked her head and murmured, "No, my lord," but she chose to titter and bat her lashes instead.

"How you flatter me, my lord," she said dramatically. "Can you see that I am not yet of age? My mother only allowed me to come tonight because I begged to be let out of the schoolroom. Lessons are such tedious affairs, are they not? Pure rubbish if you ask me. I would as lief read Radcliffe's latest novel than study French."

Rather than lose interest as she expected, Lord Knave seemed to find her declaration humorous. "I think most people would prefer to read an adventure than study French, not that they would admit it."

Oh dear. He was not supposed to think her amusing. He was supposed to think her daft. Or at the very least ridiculous.

Sophia rolled her eyes. "She is bamming you, sir. Prudence is no more in the schoolroom than I am, and she speaks flawless French. In truth, she should be making her come out this season if not for me and the wretched illness that kept me from traveling to London last year."

Their mother didn't seem overly pleased by Sophia's pronouncement, but Prudence could have hugged her sister for not allowing her to remain silly or naïve or overlooked. It wasn't that Prudence wished for Lord Knave's good opinion, but she did not like pretending to be something she was not. It felt dishonest and wrong and did not sit well with her. But her sister had set it all to rights, and in so doing, revealed her own integrity. If Lord Knave did not find that trait admirable, he was both a knave *and* a nincompoop.

She returned the man's stare with a cool look of her own, wanting nothing more than to tell the man that he did not deserve her sister. *Your social standing might exceed hers, but* her *character exceeds yours by leaps and bounds.*

A reel was announced, and Lord Knave surprised Prudence by nodding in her direction. "Miss Prudence, would you honor me with this dance?"

Her mouth dropped open slightly, and she may or may not have uttered an incoherent squeak, but Felix's timely return with the drinks gave her a moment to gather her wits. She gratefully accepted the goblet filled with lemonade, took a long sip, and handed it to her mother before facing Lord Knave.

"I do apologize, my lord, but I have already promised this dance to Mr. Callaway."

To Felix's credit, not even a flicker of surprise crossed his features. He merely nodded and offered Lord Knave an apologetic shrug. "You must request Miss Prudence's hand in advance if you want to guarantee a dance with her." He glanced at Sophia and added, "And you as well, Miss Gifford. Do say you will join me for the following set?"

Sophia's eyes danced merrily. "I'm afraid I have already promised myself to Lord Knave for the supper dance, but I am free any dance after that one."

This time, it was Lord Knave who offered the apologetic shrug, though his bordered on smug. "It appears as though we are both doomed to disappointment, Mr. Calloway. I shall do my best to bear it with dignity. Mrs. Gifford, always a pleasure, Miss Gifford, I look forward to our supper dance, and Miss Prudence, I wish you a good evening." He bowed politely and turned away. After a brief scan of the room, he began walking in Mrs. Harper's direction, no doubt giving himself a pat on the back for doing his duty by Sophia.

Prudence had the greatest desire to toss a glass of lemonade over his head. Did the man have to be so transparent? Could Sophia not see him for the cad he was? Unfortunately, her sister now smiled at something their mother said, her attention no longer on Lord Knave.

Botheration, thought Prudence. Somehow, she would find a way to make her sister see more clearly.

Felix cleared his throat, and Prudence realized he had been holding his arm out to her, waiting for her to join him.

She quickly slipped her arm through his and allowed him to lead her onto the dance floor.

"Do you still wish for me to race to your side for the supper dance as well?" he teased. "And perhaps the one after that? Careful, Prudence, or the old biddies will expect a betrothal announcement before the night is over."

Prudence cursed inwardly. Felix was right. She would have suggested that Lionel take her into supper instead, but the twins were always careful to dance only once with each lady. If Felix danced twice with a woman and Lionel danced with her again, some might mistake that for a third dance for one twin and tongues would wag. No one was ever certain which twin was which.

By asking Felix to dance a second time with her, Prudence had made sure that Lionel would not request a dance at all. Which left her with no one to save her from Mr. Winston.

Drat.

From the corner of her eye, she spotted the farmer standing at the edge of the dance floor, eying her with a look one might give a plump strawberry.

Prudence gave Felix's arm a squeeze and lowered her voice to a whisper. "I suppose I must release you from the supper dance, mustn't I? 'Tis a shame, though, as I greatly prefer your company."

Felix raised his eyebrow, watching her curiously. "As opposed to whose? Lord Knave's? Never say you find the man objectionable. I'll not believe it. But why else would you go to such lengths to avoid dancing with him?"

Prudence contemplated how to answer as she took her place for the set. At last she shrugged. "Perhaps I find him a little objectionable."

Felix's eyes widened in surprise. "How very interesting. I believe you are the only one of my acquaintance who has ever said or even thought such a thing. Most people find the man exceptional."

"Perhaps they are not as observant as I," muttered Prudence, realizing as soon as the words had slipped out that she should have kept them to herself. If Lord Knave *was* to become her brother-in-law, it would never do to put it about that she didn't care for him.

Felix opened his mouth to respond, but the music began and the steps of the dance led them apart. When they came together again, Prudence changed the subject, teasing him about his drooping cravat. He frowned and peered down at it, missed a step, and Prudence found something else to tease him about. Soon they were bantering and laughing as they always did, and all talk of Lord Knave floated away in the stifling and airless ballroom.

When the dance ended, Mr. Winston arrived at Prudence's side, reminding her that she had agreed to partner him for the supper dance, which she hadn't. But she refrained from saying as much and politely accepted his arm, telling herself that it was only one dance and one meal. And besides, her mother could never accuse her of stealing away another man's attention while in the company of Mr. Winston. The man did not know how to laugh.

As she feared, supper turned out to be an interminable ordeal. Not only did Mr. Winston have a great deal more to say on the subjects of drainage and crop rotations, but they were seated nowhere near any of Prudence's family or friends. The couple on her left were interesting enough, but Mr. Winston did not allow her to exchange more than a few pleasantries with them. He claimed her attention most thoroughly, and by the time the last course was served, her head threatened to split open.

Prudence wanted nothing more than to take an early leave, but that would require her family to do the same, and at the other end of the table, Sophia seemed to be enjoying herself. So Prudence attempted to keep her head as motionless as possible and smile as best she could.

As soon as supper ended, however, she made her excuses and fled out the side door into a room that smelled of paper and leather and heaven. The library. She smiled as she breathed in the familiar scent, feeling the ache in her head ease a bit.

Once her eyes had adjusted to the darkness, Prudence walked to a bookcase and slid her fingers along the spines, searching for a novel. She didn't care if there would only be time for a chapter or two. She needed relief, and a story would be just the thing. Unfortunately, there were no novels to be found, so she pulled out a book on astronomy and settled into a cozy wingback chair.

A few pages in, her eyelids began to grow heavy, the result of too many sleepless nights. She tried to hold them open for a time until she capitulated, thinking it best to let them rest for just a moment or two.

FOUR

PRUDENCE AWOKE TO the sound of feminine laughter.

She blinked slowly, waiting for her awareness to return, then peeked around the edge of the chair, only to duck back out of sight when she spied the profile of a woman wearing a sapphire gown throw her arms around a darkly dressed gentleman.

"Knave," the woman breathed. "How you make me laugh. What a dear you are. I know you have only just returned, but I must thank you for coming tonight. You have no idea how much I have missed you."

"And I you, Catherine. It is good to see your lovely smile again."

"It feels a bit foreign, I will admit. But seeing you has made my smile genuine again. Goodness, it has been far too long. This past year has been the longest of my life."

"A necessary evil, I'm afraid. But I am here now and here I will remain—at least until the London season commences."

"How wonderful that sounds." Her voice was hushed, warm, and seductive. Prudence pictured her trailing her fingers along the nape of his neck or threading them through his hair. According to the books she'd read, that sort of touch had the power to captivate a man—not that Lord Knave needed captivating. He had already proved he couldn't take his eyes off the woman.

"Are you feeling well enough to return now?" Lord Knave asked quietly. "If we do not go back in soon, our absences will be noted and there will be talk."

"Let them talk," she pouted. "I do not care a fig for anyone's good opinion but yours."

"You know that isn't true." Prudence could hear the smile in his voice.

"No, but I will say it nonetheless. It feels good to be a little rebellious. But go if you must. Miss Gifford will wonder what has become of you, and we can't have that, can we? You need to play the part of a besotted suitor if you are to win her hand."

"Must I?" He sighed, making it sound like the most onerous of tasks.

Mrs. Harper laughed lightly. "Yes. Now go and be your charming self. I shall wait a few minutes and sneak out the other door, then send for my carriage."

"You're leaving?"

"I have no reason to stay. You are the only person I wished to see tonight, and I have already claimed your attention for two dances. But I will meet you tomorrow morning at your hunting lodge as planned. Nine o'clock?"

"Yes." There was a moment of quiet before he added, "Are you certain you are well, Catherine? You still look a trifle pale."

"I am perfectly well. Now shoo, or both of our reputations will be in tatters. You have already wrinkled my dress most abominably. I could not return to the dance in this state even if I wanted to, which I do not."

His chuckle was accompanied by the sound of a floor board squeaking. "Until tomorrow then."

"Tomorrow," she responded quietly.

The door opened and closed as Lord Knave exited, and the room became eerily silent. Prudence tensed, attempting to remain perfectly still. Even the slightest hitch in her breath or rustle of her gown would give her away.

"Oh, Knave," came a quiet murmur. "I have missed you."

A floorboard creaked again, skirts swished, and another door opened and closed quietly. Prudence waited a moment before finally allowing herself to exhale.

She remained seated as she replayed the conversation in her mind, her jaw clenched in anger. It seemed her earlier assessment of Lord Knave had been correct after all. He *was* an unscrupulous and despicable knave.

The audacity of the man! The deceit!

A plot began forming in Prudence's mind—a deliciously sinister tale about a man who led a duplicitous life. By day, he was a proper gentleman with an elegant wife and family. By night, he was a womanizing bounder. The heroine took on the likeness of her sister with vibrant red hair and a smattering of freckles dotting her cheeks. The villain, on the other hand, looked exactly like Lord Knave.

Over the years, Prudence had spent a great deal of time walking the grounds of Talford Hall. She'd even trespassed a time or two onto Radbourne Abbey and happened to know precisely where the hunting lodge stood. She'd even used it as inspiration for a cottage in one of her stories.

If she were to go there tomorrow at say, half past eight, she might accomplish two feats at once. Not only would she be able to compile actual evidence against Lord Knave's character—hopefully enough to make her sister rethink her reasons for wanting to marry the man—but she would see firsthand how a real-life assignation played out.

That information could come in quite useful with some of her stories. Prudence was certain he could teach her far more about the natures of men than Ms. Radcliffe ever could—at least the natures of despicable knaves.

HILDEBRAND CANNON, OTHERWISE known as The Viscount Knave, or simply Knave to his closest friends and Brand to a few select others, dismounted and tied his horse to a post near the front of his family's hunting lodge. He examined the sandstone structure, thinking it should look different. Older and aged, perhaps. Crumbled. It seemed like ages since his good friend, Stephen Harper, had taken that fatal fall from his horse in the woods to the west of where Brand stood. Only a year ago, Stephen had sat on his horse at Brand's side, goading, teasing, and proposing ideas for various larks. Within the short span of several minutes, Stephen had gone from his vibrant, boisterous self to a silent and broken man, never to laugh or breathe again.

One slip of a hoof, one fall, and Catherine had lost her husband and Brand his best friend—all because Brand had decided to host an impromptu hunting excursion.

How dark that time had been. He still remembered the day of the funeral so clearly. Not a single cloud marred the sky, but the air around him had felt dark and oppressive, as though a thick canopy of clouds suffocated him.

The all-too-familiar pain struck him in the chest, and he clenched his jaw. He should not have agreed to come. Far too many memories enshrouded this place—too many reminders of good times that would never be had again.

Brand should have remained in London where it had been easier to forget and not feel. He'd surrounded himself with friends concerned only with entertaining themselves and had spent the last year caught up in frivolous pursuits like gambling, boxing, horse racing, and women. He would have continued in that vein if not for his blasted sense of duty. Not only had Catherine begged him to return, but the time had come for him to renew his courtship of Miss Sophia Gifford.

Brand closed his eyes and shook his head. He wasn't ready for this. He wasn't ready to face the past, stick his neck in the parson's noose, or follow in the footsteps of his responsible father.

He wasn't ready for anything.

Why couldn't it have been him who had died instead of Stephen? Brand didn't have a beloved wife to leave behind— a woman who, bless her soul, had never once blamed Brand for the accident that had claimed her husband's life.

But Brand had. He probably always would.

From somewhere up above, a sneeze sounded, followed by a muttered feminine oath. Brand peered up at the large sycamore tree towering overhead. A single piece of paper floated down towards him, tossing this way and that as it scraped against a few leaves and branches, landing on the dirt path near his boots. He picked it up and scanned the page briefly before peering up once more. Through the foliage above, he spied some purplish-blue fabric and caught a glimpse of what appeared to be a straw bonnet before it disappeared behind a section of dense foliage. He waited a moment, but no further sounds were heard.

"Catherine?" he asked, even though he knew it couldn't possibly be her. Not only did Catherine have a great fear of heights, but she wouldn't feel the need to hide in a tree when her presence had been expected. But who else could it be?

No answer came, which confirmed that the woman in the tree was most certainly not Catherine. Who then? A servant? A runaway? A poacher?

He looked down at the page he held in his hand, studying it more closely. An elegant script covered the entire page.

Christiana crept into the woods, her heartbeat escalating with every snap of a twig, tweet of a bird, and rustle of leaves. The sound of an axe striking a tree with slow and deliberate movements came from somewhere in the distance. Her feet stilled for a moment as she attempted to collect her breath and gather her wits. Then she moved forward once more, away from the sound of the axe and towards the dilapidated hunting lodge located in the southwestern corner of the property.

Would she find the area empty and vacant, or would her suspicions be confirmed by the sight of her husband with another woman? A small part of her hoped she'd catch him there because it would mean her imagination had not carried her away into madness. The other part of her, the one that wanted to believe her husband loved her even though he had never given her a reason to believe as much, hoped she had been wrong.

The sound of her husband's voice met her ears, and Christiana's body stilled. She carefully slid a branch of a large elderberry bush aside. Across a small clearing, she saw the back of his charcoal black head. His neck, however, was surrounded by two feminine arms clothed in peach muslin.

Christiana might have gasped if not for the sudden dryness in her throat.

No, no, no.

Her husband spoke again, and this time she heard him clearly.

Brand turned the page over, but there were no additional words on the other side. He pursed his lips and glanced up into the tree once more. Who was up there? If it was the woman who had authored this page, her prose and elegant hand indicated that she had been well educated. But what well-educated woman—or was it a girl?—would hide away in a tree on his family's property?

A woman who did not wish to be discovered, judging by her continued silence.

"You must not keep me in suspense," said Brand in a conversational tone, slowly stepping to the side in an attempt to get a glimpse of her face. "What did the man in your story say?"

As expected, no answer came. Not to be deterred, Brand tried again, hoping to apply to her vanity. "In only a few short paragraphs, you have captured my interest." She needn't know that he was referring to her and not her story. "Come now, I must know."

Still no answer.

"Perhaps you have not figured out what he should say. Is that it?" Brand speculated. "In that case, I can probably be of assistance. The woman wearing peach is obviously his aunt. Her poodle of nine years only just passed away, and her kind and thoughtful nephew, whom she adored like her own son, whisked her away from the miserable scene and led her on a walk about the grounds. When she couldn't contain her grief any longer, she threw her arms around him and sobbed into his shoulder. It's a tender moment, and his only response can be, 'There now, Auntie. Everything will come about all right. You'll see.'"

A scoff sounded from the leaves, making them quiver a bit. Brand smiled a little. This exchange was proving to be as interesting as it was unexpected.

"Am I to take it that he has no aunt then? Hmm . . . Perhaps it *is* an unscrupulous woman, luring the husband to the scene with a note containing concerns of a serious threat on her life. When he arrives to rescue her from some nefarious snake, she throws herself upon his person with the hope of seducing him. He is momentarily stunned, of course, but will soon say, 'What the devil are you doing?' and cast her away."

"You are wrong," came a lovely, melodious—and *familiar*—voice that sounded like it belonged to a young woman. "He does not say or do anything of the kind. He is a despicable man who has made an assignation with a woman who is not his wife."

Apparently Brand had touched upon a nerve that could not be quieted. Good. He tried to place where he'd heard that voice before, but his mind drew a blank.

He took another step to the side, trying to get a better look. "Pray tell, what *does* he say?"

"Perhaps you should tell me, sir."

Her words, spoken with censure, gave Brand pause. It almost sounded as though she were accusing him of being the despicable man in her story. Had the woman gone mad? She *had* climbed a tree to compose an outlandish tale.

Brand continued to move slowly about the tree, attempting to catch a glimpse of her hair, eyes, lips—anything to give him a clue as to her identity. Where had he heard that voice before?

"How should I know what a despicable man would say?" he asked.

She did not hesitate to answer. "Why are you here now, my lord, at your hunting lodge at this precise time?"

The directness of her question made him uncomfortable. She didn't sound the least bit addled. Rather, she spoke with conviction, as though she already knew why he had come—or, at least why she *thought* he had come. He took another step to the side, annoyed by the dense foliage above him. How had she managed to climb up there?

"I am meeting a friend," he said by way of explanation.

"Are you quite certain she is merely a *friend*?"

So she knew he was meeting a woman. Did she also know Catherine would be here any moment? She must. It was the only explanation. But how had she come by such information, and why did she care?

He frowned. Could the woman possibly be Miss Gifford? No. Surely he would recognize her voice, wouldn't he? Brand thought back to the previous evening, trying to remember the quality and timbre of her voice. Had it been a higher pitch or richer, like the woman's above.

Try as he might, he couldn't recall anything about the sound of Miss Gifford's voice.

Of all the people it *could* be, she was the most likely, wasn't she? They were neighbors, after all, and the hunting lodge sat close to her family's property. In addition, if she was of a jealous nature, it would also explain her censure.

Oddly enough, a spark of hope flared within Brand. Up until this point, Miss Gifford had only ever been the woman he would be expected to marry. Several years his junior, she had been in the nursery when he'd departed for school. Occasionally his family would dine with hers during one of his breaks, but she had always been exceptionally quiet. When she'd at last emerged into local society the previous summer, Brand had felt pressure from his parents to begin his courtship of her, but it hadn't taken him long to realize why so many referred to matrimony as a noose about one's neck.

While Miss Gifford could never be described as pretty, she was graceful and fashionable enough that he might have been able to overlook the ghastly shade of her hair, the freckles, her slightly pinched nose, and eyes that were a bit too far apart to be pleasing, if not for her apathy. The few times he had been in her company, she had never laughed, never spoken passionately on any subject, and had never shown even a hint of emotion.

While he loathed admitting it, even to himself, her illness had come as a blessing. Brand had needed time to get over his friend's unexpected departure and accept the fact that he must either disappoint his parents, both of whom he respected, or one day marry a lifeless woman who could never ignite any sort of passion within him.

He'd hoped that after she regained her health and they came to know each other better, his feelings would change. But at the conclusion of yesterday's dance, when conversing with her had been the equivalent of forcing a bit into a stubborn horse's mouth, Brand had been sorely tempted to walk away from the arrangement.

If only he could.

After all these years, the town and surrounding villages had learned of the understanding between the two families. The knowing looks and smiles, the subtle and not-as-subtle implications, the expectations—if Brand disengaged now, it would cause a great deal of talk, and Miss Gifford would be made to bear the brunt of it.

He had no desire to sentence her to such a fate any more than he wished to sentence himself to a tedious marriage. He could only hope that somewhere underneath her cool exterior was a woman with interests, passions, and opinions. He simply had to break through that shell and find the real her.

Perhaps now he had.

He glanced up once more, wanting the fiery, accusatory, opinionated woman in the tree to actually be Miss Sophia Gifford.

But how to make her reveal herself and come down?

"Your silence is reassuring," came the voice from above.

Brand took another step to the side, but she seemed to match his movements with shifts of her own, keeping her upper body out of sight. Could it possibly be Miss Gifford? If so, how could a voice that had been so unremarkable and forgettable last evening now sound intriguing and memorable?

She couldn't possibly be Miss Gifford.

Brand pressed his lips together, refusing to let the spark of hope die so quickly. He sauntered over to the trunk of the tree and leaned casually against it, glancing up from a new vantage point with no better luck. He folded his arms across his chest, knowing he didn't have much time. Catherine would be along soon.

"You obviously find my character wanting, but do you also believe my friend is a person of loose morals?" he asked.

"Is she?"

"No," he said firmly. The woman could believe whatever she wanted about Brand, but he would not let her besmirch Catherine's good name.

"Then why would she agree to a private assignation?"

Brand stared up into the tree. Did she really expect him to explain something of a personal nature, something he would only confide to a close and trusted friend? Even if the voice *did* belong to Miss Gifford, she was still a far cry away from becoming any sort of confidant.

He pushed away from the tree, wondering if he had been too quick to consider her fiery responses as a reason to hope. He had no wish to wed a vindictive creature any more than he wished to marry a placid one.

"Do you always arrive at conclusions without any proof or validation?" he asked.

"No proof?" she said with a scoff. "I clearly overheard a conversation between you and Mrs. Harper in the library last night. I also saw you embracing. What further proof do I need than that?"

Brand thought back on his exchange with Catherine and had to concede that the close friendship they shared could have easily been misinterpreted for something more. But hadn't the woman also heard the reason for their so-called assignation? Catherine had begged him to meet her here, hoping they could face the past together and, with any luck, finally put it behind them.

Then another thought struck. If the woman above *had* been in the library with them, she couldn't possibly be Miss Gifford. As soon as Brand had quit the room, he had spotted her speaking with her mother on the far side of the ballroom. She couldn't have been in two places at once.

Unless someone else had overheard the conversation and related a portion of it to Miss Gifford.

Gads. Who the devil was up there?

Brand was ready to climb the tree and find out, but the sound of hooves grazing the ground met his ears. He peered through the forest of trees to spy a horse and rider approaching. Catherine.

Blast.

It seemed the woman of mystery would have to remain a mystery for now. He was not about to give her the opportunity to lecture Catherine as well.

"Here comes your lady now, my lord," came a quiet voice from above. "Have a care, sir, lest you do something you'll regret."

Brand barely refrained from insisting that Catherine was *not* his lady, nor would she ever agree to a tryst. The woman above obviously did not know either of them well or she wouldn't have leapt to such a ridiculous and sordid conclusion. Perhaps she was a woman gone mad after all.

Catherine approached with a smile and pulled her horse to a stop a few strides away. "Thank you for waiting, Knave. I am unforgivably late, aren't I?"

Brand pulled his timepiece from his pocket and glanced at it. Half past nine already? Where had the time gone? In truth, he probably *would* have given up on Catherine if not for the unexpected diversion in the tree.

"You have always been adept at keeping men waiting," he teased.

She laughed. "Yes. Poor Stephen had to deal with my tardiness quite often, didn't he?"

Brand nodded, remembering all the times Catherine had kept his friend cooling his heels. The moment Stephen spotted his wife, however, all was forgiven. The two had shared the sort of love Brand would likely never experience.

Arranged marriages were rarely love matches.

"He always said you were worth waiting for," Brand said.

Her smile became sad, and the rapid blinking of her eyes testified that she had been touched by his words. She looked past him to the hunting lodge. "Was I wise to suggest that we come here, Knave? I thought it would be good for us to face the memory of him together. Heaven knows I have never been able to do it on my own. But now I'm wondering if I will ever be able to face it. How does a person forget and move on?"

Brand approached her horse and stroked its nose. "I don't think we can forget, Catherine, nor should we.

Experiences and memories—both good and bad—are an integral part of who we are. If we try to forget them, we're trying to forget a part of ourselves, and how is that a good thing? Perhaps the trick to moving forward isn't forgetting. It's learning to use those memories as a means of becoming stronger and better versions of ourselves."

Tears dampened her eyes, and she nodded, pressing her lips together to ward off her emotions. Brand knew that look. He'd seen it many times during those wretched days following Stephen's death.

"I believe you are right," she said at last. "But how do I do that?"

He clasped her hand and gave it a squeeze. "When I first spied you last evening, wearing a genuine smile and a vibrant, beautiful gown, I saw a woman changed. You are on your way, my friend. I know it."

She wiped away an errant tear and nodded. "Thank you, Knave. But what about you? Are you on your way as well? Have you finally come to accept that you are not to blame for his accident?"

Brand released her hand and moved to retrieve his horse, knowing he couldn't answer that question in the way she wanted him to. Instead, he swung up into his saddle and glanced up at the branches overhead, recalling the mysterious woman spying on them from above.

What accusations have you to fling at us now? he wanted to ask, annoyed that she had been privy to yet another private conversation. For a moment, he thought he saw a dark eye through the leaves, but it was gone in an instant.

He turned his attention back to Catherine, ready to be done with it all. "What do you say we take our leave of this wretched place and ride to the back meadow instead?"

"Yes, please," came her answer.

He urged his horse onward, and together they rode away, leaving the hunting lodge where it stood and the mysterious woman where she perched. He may not have discovered who she was or what she looked like, but Brand knew one thing. If he ever heard that rich and melodious voice again, he would recognize it instantly.

FIVE

ALL PRUDENCE HAD to show for her morning's efforts was a ripped sleeve, a scraped elbow, and the realization that she had been wrong. How she despised being wrong, especially when she had been so certain she would *not* be wrong. She had always prided herself on being a good judge of character because she noticed things that others did not, but this time her observations had led her astray. Lord Knave and Mrs. Harper had not planned a lover's tryst. They were merely two disheartened souls attempting to mourn the loss of a beloved husband and friend.

How self-righteous and condemning she must have sounded!

Prudence could only be grateful the man had not discovered her identity or he would probably rethink his plans to marry her sister. No one of sound mind would wish to marry into a family with such obtuse relations.

She walked home slowly, her thoughts scattered and torn. The story that had flowed so effortlessly in the wee hours of the morning, keeping her pencil moving at a furious pace, had come to an abrupt and disappointing halt. She looked down at the residue of graphite on her fingers and rubbed at the darkened patches of skin absentmindedly. The pencil that had been new only yesterday was now half its original size, and it had all been for naught.

Prudence slipped through the back entrance, helped herself to a slice of bread and preserves, summoned her maid, and somehow managed to make it up to her bedchamber undetected by her mother. Ruth clucked disapprovingly over the torn fabric and scraped skin, but she helped Prudence change into a new gown, tended to the wound, and tidied her hair.

"I don't know what I would do without you, Ruth," said Prudence, grateful for a maid who could be trusted to keep a level head and her mouth shut. Only a few years older than herself and much too thin, Ruth had saved Prudence from many a scrape.

This time, however, her talents could only go so far. Ruth shook her head at the torn periwinkle sleeve. "I don't think I can mend this, miss, least not without it lookin' mended."

Prudence eyed the shredded fabric with a frown before brightening. "I have always wished that gown had shortened sleeves. Don't you agree that such an alteration would improve its appearance?"

Ruth snickered, gathering the dress in her frail arms. "Aye, miss. That I do. I'll see what I can do."

As soon as her maid had left the room, Prudence carefully lifted the floorboard near her bed and grabbed the small stack of foolscap she had covered with her scribblings during the night. The pages contained the beginning of the story about the deceitful and unscrupulous man and his sorrowful wife—a story Prudence had no desire to finish any longer. Before she could talk herself out of it, she tossed every last page into the fireplace and watched the edges curl and burn until there was nothing left but ash.

It was a disheartening sight, but only because of the hours she'd wasted writing it. Thanks to the tender exchange between Mrs. Harper and Lord Knave, her mind had been turned to something new and better. She no longer wanted to write about an unfaithful husband. She wanted to write about the kind of love Mrs. Harper had spoken about with such pain and reverence—the kind that was as rare as it was beautiful. Only Prudence's story would not end in sadness as Mrs. Harper's had. It would conclude with joy and wonder and endless possibilities—a tale that could inspire even the most unromantic soul to want more from a marriage than a title and wealth.

Prudence snatched her shawl, replaced her bonnet, and escaped the house undetected once more. Clouds had scattered across the sky, threatening to hide the sun now and again, but she ignored them. A new plot had begun to form, and her mind whirled with ideas of scenes, conversations, antics, and thoughts. She loved it when her mind came alive in this way.

She crossed a wide meadow, meandered through a thicket of trees, and emerged onto the lane. She was vaguely aware of the sunlight beaming and hiding, birds flying overhead, and sheep grazing in the distance. Her feet scraped the grass and dirt as she walked and thought, wishing she had brought her pencil and paper with her.

At long last, sounds of an approaching carriage intruded, and Prudence glanced over her shoulder to see a gig begin to slow. As soon as she spied Lord Knave and her sister, she panicked. Would he recognize her from that morning? No, she had taken great pains to remain hidden, and she now wore an apricot afternoon dress instead of the torn periwinkle. But there was a definite possibility that he would recognize her voice.

She lifted her chin and greeted them with nothing more than a smile.

Sophia looked down, her brow creased in surprised confusion. "Prudence, where have you been? Mama has been searching the house and grounds for you all morning, but no one knew of your whereabouts, not even Ruth."

Prudence glanced at Ruth perched at the back of the gig and offered her an apologetic look. Then she lowered her voice in an attempt to disguise it. "I'd best be on my way then. Good day to you both."

"Are you ill?" Sophia persisted. "Your voice sounds . . . odd."

The sun came out of hiding, and Prudence squinted into it. She cleared her throat and tried to make her voice sound a little more normal, but not quite. "I'm just a trifle parched is all. Nothing to worry about. Good day."

She didn't take more than a few steps when her sister's voice came again. "You have traveled rather far. Would you like a ride home? It is half past two already."

Half past two? Prudence's eyes widened in surprise, and she glanced at the sky, noting the sun's location in the western sky. Oh dear. No wonder Sophia seemed on pins and needles. How in the world would Prudence explain her lengthy absence to her mother? Would she believe her daughter had gone for a walk and lost her way?

Not likely. Prudence knew the land far too well.

"I, er . . ." Prudence eyed the gig, thinking a ride would be most welcome. Her feet ached, and the sooner she returned home the less time she would be required to explain away. But the contraption only seated two people comfortably, and it would be far worse for Prudence if she was seen disrupting an outing between Lord Knave and her sister. Her mother would never forgive her that.

"Thank you, but I'd prefer to walk." Too late, Prudence realized she'd forgotten to disguise her voice. She bit her lip and glanced at Lord Knave, noting with chagrin the spark of recognition that appeared in his eyes.

Confound it all, she thought to herself as she began to walk away, only to be halted by his voice.

"Tell me, Miss Prudence, have you been out and about all day?"

She eyed him with suspicion, wondering what sort of information he was hoping to uncover. She wasn't about to admit that she had climbed a tree and lectured him from the treetops that morning. He may *think* he recognized her voice, but he couldn't be certain, could he? She'd probably only imagined his recognition.

"For most of it, yes," she answered.

He glanced at her gown and pursed his lips in thought before saying cryptically, "Have you changed gowns since this morning?"

Prudence nearly coughed. Drat. He *did* think it had been her, otherwise he would have never asked such a question. Sophia looked at him oddly but didn't say anything.

Prudence bit her lip. Should she lie? The thought twisted her stomach in an uncomfortable fashion. She hated outright lying—it pricked at her conscience in a displeasing way and never failed to complicate matters. But if she told the truth, what would he ask next? Would he inquire as to the color of gown she had been wearing earlier? What would she say then?

Prudence settled on a vague answer. "A woman often changes clothing multiple times a day. There are morning gowns, promenade dresses, visiting gowns, walking gowns, carriage dresses, riding habits, dinner gowns, ball gowns—"

"Honestly, Pru, do you think Lord Knave cares about such things?" interrupted Sophia, her face slightly pink from embarrassment.

Prudence could only hope that she had bored Lord Knave into forgetting his line of questioning. Unfortunately, he appeared more amused than anything. "Actually," he said in a conversational tone, "I had no idea a woman's wardrobe contained such a wide diversity of gowns. However do you keep them all straight?"

"We don't," said Prudence, pleased by the shift in conversation. "Ruth does that for us."

Lord Knave followed Prudence's gaze to the maid seated on the back of the gig. He shifted in his seat to better see her. "Ah yes, your maid. Forgive me, Ruth, I had almost forgotten you were with us."

Ruth shot him a look of surprise. "A maid's suppose ter be forgotten, milord."

"I disagree," he said. "No one, be it a maid or a queen, should ever be forgotten." With those few words, the man had effectively turned Ruth up sweet. Prudence could see it in the rosy hue to her cheeks, her bashful smile, and the slight ducking of her head.

Whatever was the man about?

"Tell me, Ruth," he continued. "Do you have a great deal of washing to do every day?"

She giggled and nodded her head. "Aye, milord, and mendin' too. Why, only this mornin' Miss Prudence tore the sleeve of her walkin' gown, and I had ter—" Ruth stopped suddenly when she noticed Prudence's glare. Her cheeks turned a fiery red, and she quickly dropped her gaze to the ground, no doubt berating herself for saying too much.

Prudence wanted to berate her as well even though she knew it would be unfair. As much as she wished the maid's words had gone unsaid, how could she blame the girl? She had been placed in the uncomfortable position of being addressed—and complimented—by a handsome viscount. Any woman in her position would have been disconcerted.

Really, the person Prudence ought to berate was Lord Knave himself, especially now that he appeared altogether too pleased with himself.

He turned his attention to Sophia. "Tell me, Miss Gifford, do you enjoy writing?"

Sophia blinked in confusion, understandably perplexed by the man's strange and seemingly unrelated questions. "I enjoy penning letters to family and friends. Is that what you mean?"

"What about stories? Do you also enjoy spinning a tale?"

"I do not. Why do you ask?"

He leaned forward and gathered the reins into his hands, cocking his head to look at both women. "The most perplexing thing happened to me only this morning. I discovered a partially written tale about a man who, bless his soul, had made the mistake of marrying a woman with a highly suspicious nature." Though he spoke to Sophia, his eyes twinkled at Prudence when he referred to the woman in the story.

She attempted not to glare at him even though she desperately wanted to. A woman of a suspicious nature? *Her?*

Perhaps she had arrived at an incorrect conclusion in the library, but she had not arrived there without good reason. How many men took a beautiful woman into a secluded room and planned to rendezvous at a hunting lodge for an innocent purpose? And they had embraced as well! It had been a compromising situation no matter their intentions. Lord Knave ought to be grateful it had been her in that chair and not some gossip.

Sophia didn't appear overly pleased with him either. "Do you think me capable of writing such a tale, sir?"

"Not necessarily," he said, unperturbed. "I simply found the page near the edge of our property lines and wondered if it could be you. It was written in an elegant hand and, if I could be considered a passable judge of the written word, was fairly well crafted."

The compliment took Prudence by surprise, and she found herself bereft of words. He had thought her words well crafted? Truly? She'd expected him to be shocked that any woman could have such unnatural thoughts, let alone record them. But no. He made it sound as though she had a particular talent for it. Did he mean it?

No. Surely not. He was merely goading her or attempting to extract more information.

"Perhaps the woman in the story was patterned after your sister," said Lord Knave, still addressing Sophia but glancing at Prudence with a hint of a smile. "Does she not appear highly suspicious at the moment?"

"My sister?" Sophia had never appeared more flabbergasted. "Are you now implying that *she* could have written such nonsense? Because I assure you that she did not. She might enjoy reading novels on occasion, but she would never write one."

"Indeed." He mused, his expression showing his surprise.

Prudence stiffened as a disconcerting thought struck. Lord Knave was now privy to something she had never told another soul. What did he plan to do with the information?

Sophia looked at him with a quizzical eye. "Sir, are you well? You seem a bit . . ."

When her sister's voice trailed off, Prudence was quick to say, "Addled?"

Sophia glared at her. "I was going to say 'not yourself.'"

Lord Knave didn't try to hide his amusement. His eyes sparkled merrily. "On the contrary, Miss Gifford, I have never felt more like myself. Do not say you find me peculiar."

"I . . ." she spluttered, clasping her hands on her lap in an uncomfortable gesture. "I do not know what to think, my lord. Perhaps it is I who is unwell."

Prudence very much wished to ring a peal over Lord Knave's head. Her sister had not noticed the humorous gleam in his eyes and didn't realize he'd been teasing her. As a result, he'd embarrassed Sophia, causing her complexion to clash abominably with her hair.

Prudence sent him a chilly look. *Say something to correct what you have done, sir, or I shall . . .* Well, she did not know what she would do precisely, other than accuse him of being a knave yet again, only for different reasons this time.

He seemed to understand her silent glare and cleared his throat. "Forgive me, Miss Gifford. I was only jesting. You most definitely are not unwell. In fact, I have never seen you look more well. You ought to blush more often. It is most becoming on you."

Prudence barely refrained from rolling her eyes, and might have, if not for the snicker that escaped her sister's lips.

"You're doing it much too brown, my lord. Blushes have never become me, nor will they ever," answered Sophia frankly. "But I thank you nonetheless."

Prudence nodded in approval at Lord Knave. Not only had his exaggerated praise distracted Sophia from her embarrassment, but it had given her something to laugh about as well. *Well done, sir,* she thought.

Perhaps he would make her sister a good match after all,

assuming he remained silent on the subject of her writing. What had he done with that page she'd dropped? Burned it? Tossed it out with the table scraps? Tucked it away somewhere safe with the intent to blackmail her at some point?

Hmm . . . that could make for an interesting beginning to a story.

No. She would not think about another story at this moment. She had already let her mind run away far too long this afternoon.

"Will you both be attending Mr. and Mrs. Beckham's soirée on Friday next?" Lord Knave's voice intruded.

Prudence nearly nodded until she realized this was the first she'd heard of the dinner party. Her brow puckered. "I'm not certain. Do you know anything about it, Soph?"

"Yes," Sophia said. "Mother showed me the invitation the other day, and I saw her write our acceptance. We will be there, Lord Knave."

Prudence nodded absentmindedly, thinking it odd that this was the first she'd heard of the invitation.

"Are you certain we cannot return you to Talford Hall?" Sophia asked, no doubt ready to resume her ride.

"I'm certain," said Prudence. "Mother will be displeased with me no matter when I return, and I have disrupted your drive long enough." She waved them off with a bat of her hand. "Please continue enjoying this delightful day. I shall take the shortcut through the woods and prepare myself for a sound lecture."

Lord Knave chuckled and tipped his hat. "I shall see you Friday next then. Good day, Miss Prudence."

Prudence watched them drive away and had to wonder at Lord Knave. Only this morning she had been certain of his sinister character, but now . . . well, now she didn't quite know what to make of him. He had mourned the loss of a good friend and showed a great kindness to Mrs. Harper. He had not berated Prudence for trespassing or for falsely accusing him. He had not made her feel unworthy for penning a silly tale. And he had not given away her secret.

Was Lord Knave the sort of man her sister could grow to love?

She was beginning to think he very well could be. The hope brightened her spirits and lightened her worries about her sister. Perhaps Sophia's unlucky circumstances were not so unlucky after all.

SIX

"PRUDENCE EDITH GIFFORD, where on earth have you been?" came her mother's voice from the parlor. It echoed through the foyer in a foreboding, spine-tingling way.

Prudence sighed, squared her shoulders, and walked into the room to find both of her parents already seated—her mother on the settee and her father on the large, brocade chair next to the fireplace, neither looking very pleased. The room was decorated in greens and yellows, and Prudence had always thought of it as a cheerful room. Today, however, it felt cheerless.

She mustered a smile. "Father, how wonderful to see you. When did you return?"

"From my journey or from my extensive ride around the estate, searching the grounds for you?" His deep voice resonated through the room, carrying with it none of its usual warmth and fondness. The worry lines that creased her father's forehead, in addition to his receding gray hair, made him appear two decades older than his wife even though only ten years separated them.

Prudence experienced a stab of guilt that she had been the cause of some of those lines. Perhaps all of them.

"Forgive me, Father," she said, adding quickly, "and

Mother. But I could not resist basking in this beautiful day. I'm afraid I lost all track of time."

"Lost all track of time?" cried her mother. "That is your excuse? Your father and I were beside ourselves with worry thinking you had been snared by a trap, attacked by wild dogs, or had befallen some other dreadful fate. And now we are to understand that you simply lost all track of time? Are you in earnest?"

Her father's lips pressed into a thin line, and his expression became quite grim. Prudence had never seen him in such a state. Her mother was often distressed by Prudence's somewhat wild behavior, but her father, never. He had always doted on her.

Until now.

For that, Prudence was sincerely sorry. Not only should she have left word of her whereabouts, but she shouldn't have allowed her mind to carry her away for so long. It had been unfeeling and selfish. She could not blame either parent for being distressed.

Prudence sank down on the chair next to her father and clasped his hand between both of hers. "Papa, Mama, I truly am sorry. Do say you will forgive me."

Her earnestness seemed to appease them a little, at least her father. Her mother threw her hands into the air in a gesture of exasperation.

"I cannot make sense of you, child. You are confident and converse well with others, and those who are acquainted with you call you charm itself. But in the confines of our home, you gravitate towards solitude and are constantly lost to whatever thoughts wander through your mind. But you have never taken yourself off with such careless abandon as you did today. What is it that occupies your mind so completely?"

Prudence swallowed and released her father's hand, moving hers to her own lap. How could she possibly explain without revealing certain truths they would never wish to hear? Despite her many fallouts and misunderstandings with her mother, Prudence did love and respect her, and she adored her father. She had no desire to say anything that would disappoint either of them, but that's precisely how they would feel if she ever told them about her deeply-rooted longings.

But she had to say *something*. They deserved some sort of explanation.

"I . . ." Prudence began, thinking frantically. "I suppose you could say that I am feeling a little lost of late. I used to fill some of my spare time with an interesting book, but now—"

"You mean *all* your spare time," corrected her mother.

Prudence had to concede the truth of her mother's words—almost. "Perhaps more than I should have, I will admit. But now . . . well, now I am not quite sure what to do with myself. I went out today with the hope of figuring some things out, and I really did lose sight of the hour." She hoped her answer did not stray too far from the truth. It had been a stretch, yes, but not entirely false.

Her father sat up straighter in his chair, and the grooves in his forehead faded somewhat. His lips pursed together in thought before he brightened and slapped the arm of his chair. "I think I have a solution."

Prudence stared at him in confusion. A solution to her distraction? She could not possibly fathom what that might be. Would he propose a stricter schedule for her that left no room for distractions? Did he intend to send for the doctor? Or did he plan to wash his hands of her and take her to Bedlam?

"You need a purpose in your life, do you not?" said her

father. "Something to keep your mind busy and your focus on a worthwhile pursuit. You have a great deal of energy that needs an outlet of some sort. Wouldn't you agree, my love?" He looked to his wife for confirmation, but she appeared as perplexed as Prudence felt.

"I suppose," she said slowly.

His grin widened as though he had landed upon a brilliant plan. "What you need, my dear girl, is a puppy."

SEVEN

As PENANCE FOR disappearing all day, Prudence was sentenced to remain at home until she could prove to be more responsible, which meant no more dances, dinner parties, picnics, or outings to town. She could walk about the grounds, practice the pianoforte, and improve her watercolors, French, and needlepoint, but that was all.

Prudence quickly grew to feel quite stifled, which affected her thinking as well. The story she had been bursting to write felt trapped in her mind the way she felt trapped at Talford Hall.

Goodness, her imagination was a finicky thing.

It was with great relief that her father at last followed through on his promise to procure her a puppy. One look at the little Yorkshire terrier, and Prudence's heart melted. Lively and mischievous, the creature scurried around her bedchamber, burrowed beneath her bed clothes, and nibbled on her fingers. Prudence wanted to give him the perfect name, but try as she might, she couldn't come up with a single word that suited him. Mischief described him well, but it would never do for a name, nor Trouble either. Chaos sounded too extreme, although the pup did cause a fair amount of it whenever he escaped the room, tripping up servants and attempting to jump on the furniture.

She supposed Rogue might fit him best, but it still was not quite right.

Hmm ... She would have to think upon it further.

As her parents had hoped, other distractions—namely, her stories and scribbling—were set aside as her mind became consumed with naming the puppy and training it to not leave puddles or other unpleasant things in her bedchamber. On one occasion, he even had the temerity to wet her mother's Persian rug. Thankfully, Mrs. Gifford had not been at home to see it happen and failed to notice the spot that one of the maids had scrubbed and scrubbed.

Prudence couldn't help but smile every time she walked into that room and saw the rug. She rather liked having "a purpose" as her father had called it. The puppy had most definitely given her life an added something.

But her scribblings would not be placed on the shelf forever. They were too much a part of her, and in time, she began to devise a plan to weave a sweet puppy into her story. Perhaps her heroine could find a haggard little creature at the side of the road and save him from starvation.

Yes, that could work quite nicely. She smiled, feeling some of her previous excitement about her most recent story return.

"See what wonderful inspiration you are?" she said softly to the puppy, lifting it up to nuzzle its nose with her own. Then she tucked the wriggling ball of cream fur to her chest and went in search of her mother and sister, finding them both ensconced in the parlor, working on their embroidery.

"Good morning, Mama. Sophia," she said as she sat on a chair across from them. "How was the soirée last evening?"

"Must you ask? I'd prefer not to discuss it." Sophia set her embroidery aside and moved to steal the puppy from

Prudence's lap. Sophia adored animals of all kinds and could never resist the newest addition to Talford Hall.

"How's my dear little creature this morning, hmm . . .?" she asked. "Still no name?"

"Afraid not," said Prudence dismissively, more concerned about her sister's obvious frustration with the dinner party. "Was it not enjoyable? I have heard much about the extravagance of the Beckham family's annual soirée. According to Mrs. Mottle, a few years ago they released a trained pigeon in the house to swoop around the room during the final course."

"Yes," said their mother with a smile. "I remember that evening well. The pigeon swooped once or twice, frightened many of the guests, then landed directly on top of Lady Spencer's coiffure. She made quite a fuss, and the Beckhams have not allowed a pigeon in their home since. But even without a bird, the evening was quite elaborate. They hired a French chef and served the most delicious food I have ever tasted."

"It was indeed elaborate," agreed Sophia, not looking nearly as pleased. "It was me who was lacking. I wish you could have come with us, Pru. Your presence would have helped immensely."

"Nonsense," insisted their mother. "Sophia, honestly, I do not know how you come by such notions. Your sister's presence is not required for you to be at ease in the company of others."

"I was certainly not at ease last night," said Sophia.

"What happened?" asked Prudence. "Was Lord Knave unkind to you? You seemed in complete harmony with him when I came upon the two of you out driving the other day."

"Yes, but only for the duration of our visit with you," said Sophia. "The moment you walked away, everything became uncomfortable again. I never know what to say to that man."

Prudence pressed her lips together, wishing she knew how to help her sister. She had never been inflicted with the same problem and could not comprehend what caused Sophia to grow so timid at times. For Prudence, there always seemed to be endless topics to discuss and not enough time to discuss them—except when in the company of Mr. Winston.

"What are his interests?" she finally asked her sister.

Sophia's brow puckered. "I cannot say for certain, although I do remember him mentioning that he used to enjoy a good hunt."

"Used to?" asked Prudence. "He doesn't any longer?"

Sophia shrugged. "He only mentioned it once, and it seemed forward of me to inquire further."

Forward? Prudence thought, confused. How could such a question ever be considered forward? Interested, perhaps. Curious, obviously. But not forward.

Their mother must have thought the same, for she said, "That is a perfectly acceptable question to ask, dearest. If he seems hesitant in his answer, then by all means, cease questioning him. But how else are you to get to know him if you do not ask about his pursuits or opinions on various matters?"

For once, Prudence and her mother were in complete agreement. It felt good.

Sophia combed her fingers through the puppy's thick fur. "I suppose you are right, but . . . I know nothing about hunting, and the question could easily lead to a discussion about a sport I am not prepared to discuss."

Prudence might have rolled her eyes if she hadn't grown accustomed to Sophia's lack of confidence in herself. "Simply tell him you know very little about hunting and ask him to enlighten you. I think most men would enjoy a captive audience."

"Indeed," agreed their mother.

Sophia sighed. "You always make it sound so easy, Pru, but it is never easy for me, especially when it comes to Lord Knave. He intimidates me."

"Not to worry, my dear," comforted their mother. "That discomfort will pass in time. It always does."

"Perhaps a brisk walk will cheer you up," suggested Prudence. She rose and collected her puppy from her sister's arms and kissed its nose. "This little troublemaker and I are planning to take a walk about the grounds, assuming we have Mother's permission." She turned the puppy towards her mother and wiggled her brows expectantly. Ever since her unhappy encounter with her parents, Prudence made an increased effort to seek her mother's permission before venturing out of doors.

As hoped for, her mother smiled a little and nodded. "Very well. You may go."

"Would you care to join us, Sophia?" Prudence asked.

Her sister appeared to consider the offer before shaking her head. "I have been attempting to finish this pillow for weeks and am determined to finish it today. I'm afraid you will have to go without me."

Prudence took a step towards the door. "If you change your mind or wish to take a break, you can find us in the wilderness area just past the gardens. It appears a bit breezy, but otherwise perfectly lovely."

"I'm sure it is. If I finish in a timely manner, I will be glad to join you." Sophia turned her attention back to her embroidery and jabbed her needle through the cloth.

Amused by her sister's determination, Prudence quit

the room and waited in the great hall for a servant to fetch a leash for the puppy. Once secured, she left the confines of the house behind and allowed her puppy to hop down the stairs and roam as far as its restraint would allow. The breeze tickled her neck, whipped at the loose strands of her hair, and lifted her spirits.

There was something wonderful about being out and about. Whether it was the freedom she always felt or the aroma of flowers and grass and earth, Prudence couldn't say. She only knew the feeling was a balm to her soul, and she never tired of it.

Earlier rains had dampened the ground, but she didn't mind. She had worn her sturdy pair of boots that navigated the soft and muddied earth with ease.

"What about Snowball for a name?" she asked her puppy. "I do so love the whiteness and irregularity of snow. And you do appear a bit like a furry snowball, especially when you curl up on my lap. But then, Father did say your fur would likely darken into a tan as you age, so perhaps not. That, and you aren't the least bit cold-hearted, are you?"

Prudence sighed. "I'm beginning to think I should not be so concerned about finding a fitting name for you and simply call you something that doesn't hold any specific meaning, like Sam or Charlie or . . . Winchester." She watched as her puppy strained against its leash, trying with all its might to run ahead. "I suppose we could call you Win for short, since it appears as though you do like to win. Oh, there I go again. I suppose I could never call you just any name, but Winchester is not it either, I'm afraid. It is far too staid, and you are too much of an imp. Hmm . . . Imp. Could that work? It could be short for Imperial, I suppose. Despite your small size, you seem to have an air of importance about you."

The puppy sniffed at the ground near a dogwood bush, paying his mistress no mind.

"I really must come up with a name soon, so I can call you to attention. It isn't the acceptable thing for you to ignore your mistress, you know."

They passed through the formal gardens and into the denser area of their property, where pines, dogwoods, and oak trees climbed high into the heavens. Although the canopy of leaves and branches made the air chillier, there was something magical about being in this forest. It felt as though creatures, the likes of which no human eyes had ever beheld, were ducking just out of sight and the trees could come alive at any moment.

Prudence briefly contemplated writing about such creatures but quickly dismissed it. She could not allow her mind to think on another tale just yet. She must make some progress on her current story first—the one that had occupied her mind with such intensity that glorious afternoon when time passed in a flurry.

She knew what she wanted to happen, what direction it would take, and how it would end. She knew she wanted to portray a deep and abiding love, the devastation involved in losing that love, and the process of healing and learning to love again. Several scenes had already been written in her mind, a few tender, a few humorous, and a few awkward. But every time she pulled out a fresh sheet of foolscap, the beginning eluded her and she had yet to write a single word. She needed to portray the heroine as deeply in love, but what did that emotion feel like? What sensations might she experience? How did it feel to embrace or kiss a man?

Prudence could imagine a great many things, but this, she did not know.

What she needed was another novel to research. She

had read many to date, but for the life of her she couldn't remember how the author had described a kiss or a touch. If only her mother would relent and allow her to read at least a little.

Prudence drew in a deep breath of fresh air and continued following her puppy through the woods. The breeze seemed to quicken, quaking the leaves overhead and stirring the bushes. She wrapped her arms to her chest, wishing she had thought to bring her pelisse, or at the very least, her shawl.

The bark of a dog echoed up ahead, and her puppy immediately lunged in the direction of the sound as though he intended to act as her protector. He even attempted his own little bark—well, more of a yip, really. It was a darling noise that sounded anything but threatening.

"I think you could use a name that will help you sound more intimidating. What would you think of, say . . . Tempest? No, that won't do either. Goodness, what a quandary."

The puppy stretched the leash to its limits, attempting with all its might to make Prudence quicken her pace. She opened her mouth to tease him when a large, brown dog burst through some shrubbery at the end of a small clearing, startling Prudence into nearly dropping the leash. Her puppy began to bark ferociously—or at least as ferociously as a puppy could—and the enormous, brown mastiff crouched, growling menacingly.

Prudence gulped as she dragged her puppy back to her while keeping a wary eye on the beast. With slow movements, she scooped up her dog and murmured, "Calm yourself." Her heart skidded to a halt, and every instinct inside her screamed at her to run, but she worried that if she did, the mastiff would pursue them. Even in her sturdy boots, Prudence could never outrun such a beast.

She swallowed, clamping her hand over the puppy's jaw to keep it quiet. He began whining and attempting to shake her hand free, showing that he did not appreciate such treatment. With an eye on the mastiff, she lowered her voice and said, "Hush," before releasing his mouth. Much to her surprise, the little dog ceased barking.

Prudence turned her attention to the mastiff, who looked to be the size of a small horse rather than a dog. A collar surrounded its neck, which gave her some measure of hope that he had been trained not to attack innocent women and puppies. Maybe if she did not move, it would keep its distance.

"Who are you?" she said as calmly as she could muster. "I don't recall seeing the likes of you on our property before."

His growling subsided, but he continued to crouch as though waiting for the right opportunity to pounce. Prudence took a careful step back, but when he began to growl again, she paused. "Who is your master, and where is he?"

A whistle sounded, followed by a masculine shout. "Brute! Where the devil have you gone? Come here at once, you insubordinate beast."

Your master has named you well, thought Prudence before raising her voice. "If you are looking for your dog, sir, he is here, holding us captive."

Rapid footsteps approached, and Lord Knave jogged into the clearing, disheveled and out of breath. He peered first at Prudence and then at his dog, and his eyes narrowed into a glare. "What are you about, Brute, frightening young women and puppies? Have you no shame?" He jabbed his finger at the ground near his mud-splattered boots. "Come here at once."

Prudence's puppy must have wanted to scold the larger

dog as well because he began his incessant barking once more. Thus distracted, Brute ignored Lord Knave and began growling again, baring its sinister teeth. Prudence directed a sharp look at Lord Knave as she clutched her puppy closer to her chest and clamped its jaw shut again. Moments later, the mastiff ceased growling as well.

"Does he yip like that all the time?" Lord Knave asked, eying the puppy.

"Only when excessively large and ominous creatures trespass on our property."

"Us? Trespassing?" He snickered. "I'm afraid you are mistaken, Miss Prudence. It is *you* who are trespassing on *our* property."

"I think not, my lord," she said. "I have walked these woods ever since I was a child, usually in the company of my nursemaid, governess, or sister, and I have never been told that we had ventured beyond our borders. If you marry my sister, it will become yours at some point, but for now it is still ours."

"And that is your proof?" he asked. "That no one has told you otherwise?"

"What other proof do I need, sir? My nursemaid was a stickler and wouldn't have countenanced behavior as uncouth as trespassing."

"Apparently she was ignorant about our property lines as well. I, on the other hand, am not. In fact, I will confidently wager Radbourne Abbey that the very ground you are standing on belongs to my father, the Earl of Bradden. Our land steward showed me the map and walked the perimeter with me only last year. I was hosting a large hunting party and did not want to be accused of trespassing on your family's land."

His argument did seem to carry a bit more weight,

Prudence had to concede. She pressed her lips together and looked around her at the familiar trees and shrubs, the fallen log that had sat in that same spot for years. How many times had she come this way? How many times had she unintentionally trespassed?

"Where, precisely, does your land steward say the property line is?"

He gestured behind her. "About twenty yards yonder, on the other side of that small spring."

She glanced behind her, not quite ready to believe him. "Are you certain?"

"Quite."

"Hmm . . ." she said, more to herself than to him. "Forgive me for not trusting your word, my lord, but I shall have to consult with *our* land steward before I am completely convinced. In the meantime, why not think of this area as neutral?"

He smiled at her suggestion and studied her a moment before nodding. "For now, I suppose that will do. But once you realize I am right, I will require an apology from both you *and* your puppy. It is not the thing to yip at one's neighbors while on *their* property."

Her puppy yipped a few times in response, and Prudence grinned at Lord Knave. "Consider that his apology in advance."

"That sounded more like a lecture than an apology."

"Yes, well, I am still in the process of training him," she said. "I would ask for your advice on how to better go about it, but your dog doesn't seem to mind you at all, so you are obviously not an authority on the subject. Can't you make him stop looking at us in that menacing way? It is most unsettling."

"He is not my dog," said Lord Knave even as he glared

at the mastiff once more. "Brute, desist and come here at once."

The dog slowly rose to its full, intimidating height, but defied Lord Knave by remaining where he stood. Prudence decided that he wasn't as menacing as he'd first appeared. In fact, she rather liked his obstinate nature. Like her own little pup, Brute had pluck.

Lord Knave must've lost patience with the dog, for he walked over and took hold of its collar. Within minutes, he fastened a leash to it which he tied to a nearby tree. "This is the thanks I am to receive for allowing you to run free?" he muttered as he secured the knot. "Perhaps this will teach you to behave with more decorum in the future."

Prudence adjusted her puppy in her arms, grateful for its small size, and studied the larger animal. "If not yours, whose dog is he? Your father's? Mother's? Valet's, perhaps?"

Lord Knave quirked an eyebrow. "Why on earth would I be walking my valet's dog?"

"I haven't the faintest notion."

He approached her slowly, clasping his hands behind his back as he gave her a shrewd look. "If you must know, he belongs to '*my lady*.'"

Prudence felt a blush heat her cheeks at the reminder of how she had referred to Mrs. Harper the other morning from the tree. *Here comes your lady now*, she had said with all the confidence and condescension in the world. How supercilious she must have sounded.

She cleared her throat. "I suppose I may have been a tad misinformed before. Pray forgive me, my lord, even though I was given ample cause to believe as I did."

He chuckled and folded his arms across his broad chest. "It seems your puppy has learned something from you after all. You are both dreadful at apologies."

Prudence lifted her puppy up and considered it with fondness before tucking his wriggling body against her neck and shoulder and giggling when it tickled. "We do get on well together."

"How fortunate you are." Arms still folded, Lord Knave took a few steps closer, making Prudence keenly aware that he was a head taller and much broader than she.

"I'm actually surprised to find you on the ground, Miss Prudence. You seem so adept at climbing trees that I would have thought you would have scurried up the nearest one the moment you heard Brute."

Prudence's smile dwindled at yet another reminder of that humiliating morning. Could they not put it all behind them and discuss other, more neutral topics? They were standing on neutral ground after all.

"I am not as adept as you might think, my lord," she confessed. "It took me nearly half an hour to settle myself into that tree. I had to climb another and cross over to the larger one—all while wearing my least favorite morning dress, no less. It was not an easy feat, I tell you."

"You were also toting your paper and pencil, were you not?"

Drat it all, Prudence thought, annoyed with him for placing her in this awkward position and annoyed with herself for being so careless. She should never have brought her scribblings with her that morning.

She lifted her chin and met his gaze. "You are now privy to my secret, my lord. What do you intend to do with the information, aside from reminding me of it every time we encounter one another?"

"How large is this secret, exactly?" he asked. "From our last conversation, I gather your sister does not know, which makes me wonder who does."

"No one," she admitted. "My mother would be scandalized if she ever found out, my father would think it a waste of time, and my sister and friends would never understand. Please, Lord Knave, do not tell anyone. If I am to keep writing, which I simply must do, my secret needs to remain a secret."

His brow furrowed, and he took a step closer, studying her in a way that made her squirm inwardly. "Why *must* you keep writing?"

"Because I must," she blurted. Could no one understand this? "It is too much a part of me, sir. I . . . I don't know how else to explain it. Haven't you ever felt as though you were meant to do something with your life? That you were given some sort of gift or talent that must be put to use? I don't know why I have such a frivolous, and perhaps even meaningless desire, but I do, and I cannot dismiss it. What would I do with myself if my mother forbade me to imagine and create? I cannot even contemplate such a scenario. And so I *must* continue. Do you not see?"

The look he gave her was nothing short of unnerving, and Prudence found herself wishing she had not been quite so open with him. Why had she thought he might understand? No one did. No one could.

At last he spoke. "I am loathe to admit that I have never felt as strongly about . . . well, anything."

How could he not feel strongly about anything? Didn't everyone have some sort of passion, something that drove them to improve—or perhaps *prove*—themselves in some way?

"Surely you have interests, my lord."

"Interests? Yes. Passions? No."

She blinked at him, disbelieving. "Perhaps you don't know what they are. You are heir to an earldom. Do you enjoy management?"

"Not particularly, no."

"Politics?"

"I try to keep myself informed, but I consider it more of a chore."

"Hunting then. You did say you hosted a hunting party last year."

He looked away and clenched his jaw, and Prudence realized her *faux pas*. The hunting party she had so casually referred to had probably been the scene of Stephen Harper's death. Why, oh why, didn't she think before speaking?

"Pray forgive me, sir. I did not mean to—"

He raised a hand to halt her speech. "It's of no consequence. The truth of the matter is that I once enjoyed hunting more than I do now, but even before the accident, I could never claim it as a passion. Only a pastime."

He appeared troubled, as though she'd exposed a weakness in his character that he had only just recognized. The expression on his face wrenched her heart, making her wish she had kept her fervor to herself. She hadn't meant to suggest that she found him lacking in some way. On the contrary, the more she came to know of him, the more she found to like.

Prudence thought of the kindness he'd shown Mrs. Harper at the hunting lodge. He had been fully present for his friend when she'd needed him, and was that not better than having one's mind constantly filled with imaginings? Had Sophia ever needed her sister at a time when Prudence was not fully present?

Probably.

In many ways, it was Prudence who could be found lacking.

"I think," she said at last, "that you undervalue your talents and interests. You may not consider them passions, but they are valuable nonetheless. What you said to Mrs. Harper that morning in front of the hunting lodge . . . well, I thought your words heroic, my lord. In fact, I intend to have one of my heroes borrow—or perhaps steal—those same words for my next story."

His expression cleared, and he gave her half a smile. "You honor me."

She laughed. "My mother would not call it an honor, but I am glad you think so."

Lord Knave considered her a moment with a partially raised eyebrow and a glint in his eyes. "I like your candid nature, Miss Prudence, and admire your passion. I find you rather . . . refreshing."

Prudence didn't know how to respond to such praise. She had become accustomed to flattery and flippancy, not sincerity, which was precisely how Lord Knave had sounded. His expression contained no amusement, only respect and approval, but how could that be? Her frank speech and so-called passion would be frowned upon by the majority of their class.

She shifted her puppy from one arm to the other and nodded towards the mastiff, who now rested in a patch of grass. He appeared more docile and approachable now, but Prudence still had a difficult time picturing the petite Mrs. Harper managing him, especially considering the fact that Lord Knave had struggled to rein him in.

"Is that truly Mrs. Harper's dog?" she asked.

He turned to study the animal before shrugging. "In a way, I suppose. He was actually Stephen's dog in the beginning and became Catherine's only after his passing. He has been a bit of a beast ever since, I'm afraid, not that he would really do anyone harm, but he will not mind Catherine at all and that causes her a great deal of anxiety. I agreed to take him for a time and see if my coachman, who is fairly adept with animals, could temper him. Thus far, it has not helped much."

At the moment, Brute appeared more wretched than menacing, and Prudence's heart went out to the poor animal.

"Perhaps he is simply in need of a friend," she mused, more to herself than Lord Knave. Ever so carefully, she lowered her little armful to the ground and offered her puppy freedom as far as its restraint would allow. He ran straight for the mastiff, showing no fear, and began his exuberant yipping once more. Brute leapt to his feet, his rumbling bark muffling that of the puppy's. Prudence dragged the little creature back, caught him up in her arms again, and shushed him with her hand over its mouth.

"Do cease yipping, or I shall sentence you to an afternoon in Mama's company. Is that what you want?"

Lord Knave grinned wryly. "He's quite the scamp, isn't he?"

Prudence lifted her gaze slowly to his as her mind caught hold of the word "scamp." She began to play with it, trying it on and testing it out. After a moment or two, she beamed.

"My lord, you have done it! You have just given me the perfect name for my puppy, and I cannot tell you how grateful I am. He has remained nameless for days, and I had nearly given up hope." She lifted her puppy to face her. "To think I considered calling you Winchester when your rightful name is Scamp. Yes, you most certainly are a scamp, aren't you? How did I not think of that before? It is so obvious now."

When she turned her smile back to Lord Knave, he watched her with an expression she could not decipher. It was neither hard nor soft, simply something in the middle.

"You are not at all like your sister, are you?" he asked.

"Sophia?" Prudence laughed. "Sadly no, much to our mother's chagrin. I am too impulsive, fanciful, and easily distracted. Be grateful you are promised to her and not me, my lord. You are getting a far greater prize, I assure you."

He didn't respond right away, merely ruffled the fur on Scamp's head. When he spoke at last, his voice was barely more than a murmur. "Do not marry me off to your sister just yet, Miss Prudence. Although there have been a plethora of discussions about the benefits of aligning our families, we are not yet betrothed."

Prudence looked at him sharply. "You do not intend to follow through with your promise?"

He sighed and took a step back, tucking his thumbs into the pockets of his coat. "I have made no promises."

"I . . ." Prudence shouldn't have been so surprised. Sophia had said much the same thing, after all, but . . . "Forgive me, sir, but my mother speaks of your imminent betrothal as though it is a certainty. My father has mentioned something along those lines as well."

"And Miss Gifford? What does she say?"

Prudence thought over what little her sister had revealed to her. "She has been more cautious, I suppose. While I believe she would *like* it to be a certainty, she has never assumed as much."

He only nodded, his expression a combination of concern and reflection.

Prudence watched him closely, wondering at the direction of his thoughts. There was something about him that set her at ease and made her feel as though she could say or ask him anything. Maybe it was the way he had acknowledged and accepted her secret so easily or maybe it was simply him. She didn't know. She only knew that she felt comfortable speaking her mind.

"Why do you pay my sister such particular attention if you do not mean to ask for her hand? Surely you must realize that the entire town believes you are courting her with the intent to propose. Or are you only playing with her emotions? Do not say you mean to injure her, or I will . . ." She let the words trail off, not sure how to finish the threat.

He chuckled. "You will what, Miss Prudence? Challenge me to a duel?"

"Perhaps."

"And what would be your weapon of choice? Swords? Pistols? A well-aimed rock?"

Prudence shook her head. "I would choose something far more excruciating—words. Should you ever face me in battle, you will come away crippled from your own guilt and remorse."

His sonorous laughter echoed through the forest around them, and Prudence decided she rather liked the sound.

"Something tells me that I probably would," he said. "But rest assured that I have no intention of injuring your sister. The problem is that I don't know her at all. I would *like* to know her, but I have spent hours in her company and still feel as though we are strangers. When we encountered you on the road, she seemed to lower her guard a little, but as soon as we left you she became much less approachable. What you interpret as increased attention towards her is merely an increased effort to discover if we could be compatible. Call me old fashioned, but I could never marry a woman I cannot converse with easily. Unfortunately, as with Brute over there, my efforts are not amounting to much."

Prudence nodded in agreement, though she definitely wanted more from a marriage than easy conversation. She took a moment to study Lord Knave's face—his arched brows and the creases between them, the sweep of his dark hair under the brim of his hat, the determined set to his lips, and eyes the color of clouds before a storm. There seemed to be a storm inside him now, whether it was because of her sister or something else she didn't know. She only saw the telling lines and creases.

Prudence hadn't thought it possible that she would ever come to like Lord Knave, but she did. More than that, she respected his honesty, his willingness to overlook her earlier judgments of him, and his opinions on marriage and compatibility. He seemed the sort of person who would treat her sister with kindness and respect. Perhaps one day he would even grow to love Sophia the way she deserved to be loved.

If only they could get past their current awkwardness.

"Do not give up on Sophia just yet, sir," Prudence blurted. "I'm certain that if you give her a bit more time, she will surprise you."

His eyebrow raised slightly, as though he found her claim hard to believe. "Do you?"

"Yes."

His jaw clenched as he looked away, appearing no less skeptical than he did before.

Prudence pursed her lips for a moment before taking a cautious step towards him. "Perhaps I can help. She is my sister after all, and I know her better than most."

A wry smile touched his lips before he dropped his gaze to the ground and scuffed at a pebble with his boots. "How do you plan to *help*, exactly?" His tone was filled with amusement, as though he found her offer childish.

Prudence chose to disregard it because she really felt as though she *could* help. He simply needed to be around Sophia when her sister was her most comfortable self. "There is nothing Sophia loves more than racing across a meadow on the back of her horse."

The information seemed to interest him. "Now that you mention it, I noticed her out riding a great deal over the years. She's quite good."

"Yes, and she may even shock you by removing her bonnet as soon as the house is out of sight. She would never say as much, but she detests wearing bonnets. Mother thinks she comes by her freckles naturally, but I know for a fact that the sun is to blame for many of them. She adores tilting her face toward its warmth."

His twinkling eyes met hers. "You Gifford daughters certainly have your secrets, don't you?" He didn't show any signs that he found her sister's freckles—and the cause of them—unpardonable or even shocking. On the contrary, he seemed to think it charming.

"Everyone has secrets," Prudence said.

He nodded in agreement before plucking a large oak leaf from a nearby branch. He began twirling it between his fingers in an absentminded way. "So you're saying that if I can get Miss Gifford to let down her hair, so to speak, and ride with abandon, I will at last uncover the real her?"

"You will indeed."

"And if she rides with complete decorum and leaves her bonnet tied to her head?" he asked.

"Then you must tell her to cease being so prim and proper."

He laughed at that, and the sound caused Brute's ears to perk up and Scamp's pathetic little bark to begin anew. Prudence chuckled, not bothering to squelch the noise this time. It seemed a happy, non-threatening bark, and puppies were allowed to laugh as well.

Scamp began squirming in her arms, obviously wanting

to be free, so Prudence massaged its belly. "I must thank you, sir, for giving Scamp his name and for being so understanding about us trespassing on your property."

"I thought it was neutral ground."

"And so it is," she agreed, glancing around. A large oak tree extended high overhead, its beautiful bark gnarled from age, weather, and animals. Various shrubs and plants sprouted from the damp ground, some larger, some smaller. She breathed in the luscious smells of vegetation and earth, feeling perfectly content.

"I do so like this spot," she said as she faced Lord Knave once more. "Perhaps I will refrain from clarifying the property lines with our land steward for now so I can continue to enjoy its beauty. Only smell the deliciousness of these woods. Does the scent alone not energize your soul?"

The gleam in his eyes contained a confusing mixture of admiration and amusement. "I think I find the company more energizing than the scent," he said.

His words caused her heart to skitter, but she quickly squelched it. That would never do. Lord Knave may have turned out to be far more interesting than she had ever thought possible, but he was still pledged to her sister, and Prudence would see that he remained that way. She would tell him exactly how to go about courting Sophia, and in return, she would beg a small favor from him.

She shifted Scamp from one arm to the other, hoping the change would ease his growing restlessness. "Before I go, my lord, might I offer a suggestion?"

His expression showed both curiosity and wariness. "What sort of suggestion?"

She cleared her throat, attempting to sound more confident than she felt. "It is obvious you're in need of my assistance where my sister is concerned, and it just so happens that I could use your assistance as well. I was merely thinking that we could both, er . . . help each other out."

"How am I to help you, exactly?"

She rushed on to explain. "By answering any questions I might have about a man's perspective on various things."

"What sorts of things?"

"Oh, I don't know. Just . . . things. Nothing that will make you uncomfortable, of course. I only need to understand how a man might think or behave in certain situations."

He crossed his arms and leaned against the trunk of the large oak, watching her with a raised eyebrow. "Such as a married man on his way to a lover's tryst?"

She waved away his concern. "No. I have dismissed that story and am in the process of composing a . . . happier, less embittered one."

"I'm relieved to hear it."

"In fact," Prudence pressed on, "I am hoping you will introduce me to Mrs. Harper. I would very much like to ask her some questions as well."

The expression on his face told Prudence what his answer would be before he spoke the words. "You may start by questioning me, and if I determine your questions to be harmless, perhaps I will reconsider."

She nodded, respecting his desire to protect his friend. Perhaps it was for the best anyway. Prudence didn't want to cause Mrs. Harper additional pain by stirring up memories of the past, but oh, how she'd love to know the woman's thoughts on the subject.

"Do you have any questions for me now?" asked Lord Knave.

She bit her lip, knowing she needed time to articulate them better. She hadn't given much thought to her story for days, and if he was truly willing to answer her questions, she wanted to be thorough. "Give me a week, and I shall have a list of questions for you."

"A *list*?"

She dismissed his concern with a flippant wave of her hand. "Only a few pages or so, nothing too strenuous."

"Pages?"

"Yes, only two or three." She tried her best to keep a straight face, but it didn't serve. His expression was far too comical. She giggled. "I'm only teasing, Lord Knave. I promise to keep my questions to a minimum. I shall also think up more ways for you to successfully court my sister. Do we have an accord?"

Her words didn't seem to appease him, but he eventually nodded nonetheless. "Very well. Let us meet back here at the same time next week. In the interim, I will take your sister on a ride, and you can begin your list of *reasonable* questions. How does that sound?"

"My lord," Prudence chided. "Are you proposing another assignation with a woman who is not your soon-to-be betrothed? Careful, sir, or I might go back to thinking of you as a knave."

"Perhaps I *am* a knave."

"Then you are not allowed to court my sister."

He snickered. "I will keep that in mind should I decide that we are not as well-suited as some might hope. It would be an easy thing to behave as my name suggests."

Prudence attempted to glare at him, but it fell sadly short of the mark. "You are teasing me."

"Yes." He smiled. "But if you'd rather not meet me here again, you may slip me a note at the musicale on Friday, assuming you are planning to attend. Or I could call upon you at Talford Hall. I'm sure your mother and sister would not find that the slightest bit odd. Or perhaps we can invent some sort of code and exchange letters. Do you happen to know a language your parents do not? Egyptian, perhaps?"

"Do you know Egyptian?" she asked, grinning at his ridiculousness.

"No."

"Then how would you read my notes."

"I would hire a translator."

Prudence's body shook from suppressed laughter. "Do stop, my lord, or poor Scamp will think the earth is quaking."

Lord Knave pushed away from the tree and approached her, gently removing Scamp from her arms. His close proximity had an unsettling effect on Prudence's heart, but she did her best to disregard it as he held the puppy up with one large hand under its middle.

"It appears to me as though you could use some exercise," said Lord Knave to the puppy. "Shall we let you down?"

Scamp's tail waved excitedly, and Lord Knave lowered the animal to the ground, allowing it to run about their feet. Much to Prudence's relief, her little dog did not attempt to threaten Brute. Hmm . . . Perhaps he *could* be trained to mind her in time.

"I must say, Miss Prudence," said Lord Knave, wandering over to untie Brute from the tree. "I am glad you trespassed on our property today. It has been a pleasure."

"It has," she agreed.

"Until next week then." He tipped his hat in her direction before taking his leave. Brute sniffed, but made no additional noise as he trailed behind at a sedate pace.

Prudence watched them for a moment before her puppy began yipping once more. She looked down fondly and tugged gently on his leash. "Come now, Scamp. If we do not return soon, Mother will fret and worry and lecture me yet again. You have yet to experience one of her rants, so you must take my word for it that they are not at all pleasant."

Scamp barked and began to follow her in his round-about way. Prudence let him sniff and investigate various things while her thoughts returned to Lord Knave and a smile returned to her face.

EIGHT

BRAND CAST A SIDELONG glance at his riding companion. The deep blue of her habit suited her well, and her matching bonnet framed her face in an attractive fashion. But that was as much of a compliment as he could give her. Miss Gifford sat on a horse as though she had a broomstick tied to her back, appearing less than thrilled to be out riding.

After their almost painful conversation—or rather *attempt* at conversation—at the musicale a few days earlier, Brand had been hesitant to follow through on his promise to invite her for a ride. It had taken him until Monday afternoon to issue the invitation.

Now here they were, riding at a sedate pace while struggling to come up with something of interest to say to one another.

He peeked at her from the corner of his eye, trying to imagine her without a bonnet. Had Miss Prudence been bamming him about that? Did Miss Gifford really enjoy racing across the open meadow with her hair about her shoulders? Brand couldn't picture it. Nor could he picture her laughing or teasing or saying anything other than what was proper.

He halted his horse and twisted to look at her. "How would you feel about a race?" he blurted.

Her eyes widened, appearing both surprised and pan-icked. "A race?"

"Yes, it's when two people—or horses in this instance—attempt to outrun the other."

Her cheeks turned a rosy hue. "I know what a race is, my lord. I was merely surprised by the suggestion."

"Why?"

The question seemed to further discomfit her. "I don't know, exactly. I . . ." Her words trailed off, and she looked away.

Brand wondered what made her fidget and blush. Had he said or done something to cause her discomfort? Did the thought of a union between them make her as anxious as it did him? Miss Prudence had said that her sister would like to become betrothed to him, but was that true?

In an attempt to set her at ease, he mustered a teasing tone. "I'm willing to wager that my horse can outrun yours."

His words did not have the desired effect. She didn't even smile. She merely stared at him in confusion.

Untie those strings and remove your bonnet, he thought, wanting her to throw all caution to the wind and show her true self. If the woman underneath turned out to be anything like her sister, they could get on rather well together.

"I . . ." Again, her voice trailed off as her horse fidgeted beneath her.

"Do you not like to race?" Brand pressed.

"Do *you*?" she returned.

Why she felt the need to ask such a question was beyond him. Perhaps she didn't think she could admit to liking such a pastime unless he did as well, though he couldn't imagine why.

"I wouldn't have suggested it if I didn't." He smiled to soften his words.

"No, I suppose not." She surprised him by lifting her chin and looking directly into his eyes. "Under normal circumstances, I do like to race, my lord. But my horse is recovering from a minor injury, and I made a promise to our groom that I would not run him today. So a walk it must be."

He nodded, disappointed. "Perhaps another day then."

"I would like that, my lord." Her words sounded stiff and rehearsed, as though she had memorized the line and refused to deviate from it.

They continued to watch each other, and an awkward silence descended. She was the first to drop her gaze to her hands. Brand tried to think of something to say, but nothing came to mind. How was it that conversation had flowed so easily with Miss Prudence but not Miss Gifford? Although the sisters did not look alike, from what he'd observed on the road the other week, they shared an easy camaraderie. Was it him, then? Was Brand the reason he and Miss Gifford could not get past trivial pleasantries?

"What sort of injury did your horse sustain?" he asked.

"Only a sprain, or so the groom believes. I returned from a ride the other day with him favoring his front right leg. After an examination, our groom determined it was nothing serious, but I would be wise not to race him for at least a week."

"Would you like to take my horse for a run instead?" Brand asked, hoping she would accept his offer. He desperately wanted to see the other side to this timid girl—the side her sister encouraged him to discover.

She shook her head. "You are kind to offer, my lord, but I am content to take it slow today."

"Have you always liked to ride fast?" he questioned, hoping to keep her talking.

"I have." A small smile appeared on her lips. "It is one of

the few things that has come easily for me, and I cannot help but love it. The faster my horse carries me, the happier I am."

Brand smiled in return, grateful to have at last found some common ground with her. "Then it is settled. As soon as your groom feels it safe for your horse to race, we shall try again, though you'd best prepare yourself to lose."

"I shall do nothing of the kind, my lord," she said, at last showing some pluck.

Brand wanted her to say something more and continue bantering with her, but she gathered the reins in her hands and urged her horse forward, apparently thinking the conversation finished. *A pity,* he thought as he watched her move ahead. It would have been nice to see more of that pluck.

How different she seemed from her sister. Brand knew he shouldn't compare them, but he found it impossible not to do so. Miss Prudence, with her mischievous dark eyes and quick smile, was like a polished gem, shimmering and radiant. Her sister, on the other hand, seemed more like the unpolished version of a similar gem, not as shiny or sparkly, but not without potential either.

But how to bring about that transformation?

Brand had no idea. He only knew that his eyes were drawn to the more radiant sister. He liked Miss Prudence's smile, her laugh, her wit, and her candid nature. She had shredded his character from the treetops and repaired it from the ground. She had teased him in one breath and complimented him in the next. For that short while with her in the clearing, Brand had experienced a cheerfulness he hadn't felt in nearly a year. It had lightened and lifted and made him wish he could encounter her every afternoon.

Brand closed his eyes for a moment, knowing such thoughts would lead to trouble. It was the unpolished Miss Sophia Gifford he should be concerned with, not her sister.

He drew in a deep breath and forced his mind back to the woman riding ahead of him. Though she appeared more relaxed than she had in the beginning, her back remained straight, and her bonnet still remained securely affixed to her head.

Time, he thought as he prodded his horse to follow. *I simply need to give it more time.*

BRAND FOUND BOTH of his parents in the library with their heads bent together over a small table. They were an attractive pair—his father, the Earl of Bradden, with his tall stature, firm jaw, and distinguished graying hair, and his mother, Lady Bradden, with her sharp, intelligent eyes, dark hair, and youthful skin. According to his uncle, his father had once been the most sought-after bachelor and his mother, with her beauty and sizable dowry, the most sought-after debutante. Their union had been the talk of the ton, placing the young couple among the most distinguished and wealthy in all of England. But that was not the only thing their marriage boasted. From the moment they'd met, Brand was told, they had been mad for each other. His father had done what few men had. He had fallen in love with the right woman.

His parents looked up, spied their son on the threshold, and immediately quieted their conversation, which meant that they had probably been discussing Brand, or at least something having to do with him, as was often the case of late.

His suspicions were confirmed when he approached and spotted a map on the table between them, depicting the property lines of all the estates in Oxfordshire. Someone—

probably his father—had taken a quill and darkened the line surrounding the greatest estate, Hampstead Manor, which was located in the north part of the county. Another line had been drawn around Radbourne Abbey and Talford Hall, illustrating that if the two properties were joined, the Earl of Bradden and his family would hold claim to the largest estate in Oxfordshire.

Brand swallowed, knowing how much his father craved that distinction—how much Brand, as heir, should want it, both for himself and for future generations. His parents had always said that his choice of a bride was his to make, but it really wasn't, not if he wished to follow in his father's footsteps and marry for the sake of his position and family. Brand had only ever had one choice: Miss Sophia Gifford.

He swallowed, wondering why his valet had tied his cravat so blasted tight. He slipped his finger under the knot and attempted to loosen it. His mother seemed to notice the gesture, and lines of concern appeared across her forehead and around her eyes. She shifted positions to better face him and folded her hands into her lap.

"I was only just reminding your father that you should not feel any pressure to tie the knot just yet. You are young and still have plenty of time to make your decision."

Brand stopped tugging on his cravat, feeling some measure of relief. His mother always knew how to set his mind at ease. His father, on the other hand, did not.

"Plenty of time?" he said, obviously not in agreement with his wife. "How can you say such a thing? You know very well that you are as anxious as I am to see him set up his nursery."

"He is only six-and-twenty, dearest," she reminded him with a pat to his knee. "You did not marry until you were eight-and-twenty."

"Only because I was required to wait until you had made your bows."

Her eyes twinkled with mirth. "You are telling tales, sir. How can you claim to have waited for me when you did not know me?"

"I knew that I had yet to meet my bride."

She laughed and shook her head. "Flattery will not serve, Bradden. Admit it. You were far more interested in enjoying the life of a bachelor than settling down."

He leaned over and pressed a kiss to her cheek. "Only until I made your acquaintance, my love. The moment I saw you from across that ballroom, I wanted nothing more than to settle down."

She rolled her eyes, but she couldn't hide the joy in her expression. Brand marveled once again about how lucky his father had been to marry a woman who complemented him in every aspect. If only Brand could be so lucky.

His mother turned to him again, and with her hand still on her husband's knee, said, "Even though your father enjoys playing with the possibility of increasing Radbourne Abbey, you need not feel obligated to marry Miss Gifford if you cannot come to care for her. Your father and I would prefer to see you as happily settled as we have been."

His father frowned at his wife. "Arranged marriages are not without merit. Only think of my parents. Their union turned out all right, did it not?"

"Yes, but your sister is not nearly as happily settled, is she?"

"Only because my parents arranged for her to marry a poppycock, which Miss Gifford is not."

"Shouldn't that be for our son to determine?" said his mother with a gentle smile.

His father harrumphed in response, but he rolled up the map and slid it into a drawer, saying nothing more.

Brand thought back on his ride with Sophia. It had gone a little better than previous attempts to court her, but conversation had still taken a great deal of effort. They had not laughed once together. Did Miss Gifford even enjoy laughing, or did she consider it unseemly? Perhaps she didn't find Brand amusing.

"Hildebrand, dearest," said his mother. "What is troubling you?"

Brand disliked it when his mother called him by his full given name. Most mothers referred to their sons by their titles, as his father did, but not Brand's mother. She didn't care for his title, and she adored his given name. "It's distinguished and far more pleasing on the ears than Knave," she had told him.

Brand disagreed. He had grown accustomed to his title long ago, but he had never, and could never, grow to like Hildebrand. It rankled every time he heard it, and he wished greatly she would call him Brand instead.

She never had.

His mother changed tactics. "You never said how your ride with Miss Gifford went. Did you enjoy yourself?"

"Yes," he answered curtly, hoping it would put a stop to all talk involving his future bride or expectations. "I simply dropped in to tell you that I will be taking Brute for a walk. Crims seems to believe our daily excursions are doing him good. The beast is at last showing some signs of progress."

It was not precisely the truth. The real change had stemmed from their encounter with Miss Prudence and Scamp in the woods. Since that time, Brute had tempered and become far more manageable. When they went out for their daily walk, Brute dragged Brand to the clearing and refused to continue on until he had sniffed, smelled, and inspected the whole of it. When his efforts produced no

Scamp or Miss Prudence, only then would the dog move on. Brand found it humorous but couldn't deny that he, too, wished to encounter Miss Prudence and her puppy again.

"How long are we to have that beast?" asked his father.

Brand leaned forward, resting his hands on the back of a chair. "Until I can return him to Catherine a more mild-tempered animal. She has dealt with more than enough this past year and does not need an unruly dog as well."

"You seem to have taken a pointed interest in her since your return," said his mother carefully.

"She is a good friend, Mother. Nothing more."

She nodded slowly, but her expression conveyed both doubt and concern. "Catherine is a dear, but I don't believe she is the woman for you. You need someone with more spirit."

Brand's answering snicker contained no humor. "And you believe Miss Gifford is such a woman?"

She nodded without hesitation. "I do. I have had opportunities to observe her up close and from afar, and I believe her to be quite spirited. Did you notice how well she rides today? One might say that she rides with abandon. It's a beautiful sight. I believe that once you come to know her better she will surprise you most pleasantly."

"So I've heard," said Brand, somewhat annoyed that she had said much the same thing Miss Prudence had last week. What did they see in Miss Gifford that he did not? Was he so blind? Miss Gifford might be a spirited rider, but in every other context he would only describe her as reserved, proper, and without passion.

Perhaps his mother had mistaken Miss Gifford for her younger sister.

Brand removed his hands from the back of the chair and stood upright. "I'm sure that in time I will agree with you, Mother, but between now and then, I plan to make good on my promise to Catherine and subdue her dog."

His mother opened her mouth to say something more but seemed to think better of it and offered him a nod instead.

His father, on the other hand, wasn't as ready to let the matter drop. He rose from his chair and moved to retrieve his top hat. "I believe I shall join you on your walk, Knave. It is a pleasant day, and I could use the exercise."

Brand clenched his jaw to quiet the groan threatening to erupt. If his father accompanied him, Brand would be subjected to yet another lecture on duty and honor and the need to think selflessly about the future. *Only consider the positive influence we will have as the largest landowners in the county, the weight we will carry, and the laws we can change.* Brand had heard all of it numerous times before, especially when his mother was not around to keep his father in check.

He could already feel the clap of his father's hand on his shoulder and hear him say, "The decision is yours to make, son, but choose wisely." In other words, "Should you choose to wed someone other than Miss Gifford, you will be acting *un*wisely, and I shall be disappointed in you."

Brand loved his father. He admired him a great deal in many ways. He was a good husband, an honest man, and he treated his servants and tenants with fairness and kindness. But when it came to Brand, it often felt as though his father valued power and influence more than the happiness of his son.

No, that was not being fair. His father *did* value Brand's happiness. He'd simply convinced himself that his son would be happy with the heiress of the neighboring estate. Brand would once again be made to hear about all the lovely qualities Miss Gifford possessed and how he would be a fool to let this opportunity pass him by.

At least his father had never used "spirited" to describe her.

Brand closed his eyes, wanting to beg his father to leave him be. He needed to clear his head, not give it another reason to ache.

As though sensing his need, his mother rose and reached for her husband's hand, halting his progress. "Must you go, my love? I was rather hoping you could help me with the menu for Friday's dinner."

He looked at her in surprise before his eyes narrowed suspiciously. "You have never asked for my help with the menu."

"Yes, but as we have no plans for that evening, I thought it would be nice to invite the Giffords to dinner. You know Mr. Gifford much better than I, so I would very much like your input."

Judging by his expression, his father obviously thought the request a ridiculous one. But his mother didn't give up. She laced her fingers through his and smiled imploreingly. "Please?"

Brand nearly grinned. Despite his father's posturing, he could never say no to his mother. She was well aware of the influence she had on him and had used it to free her son from another lecture. Brand could have hugged her for it.

His father glanced at his son and sighed. "I suppose our walk will have to wait for another day, Knave. Enjoy your solitude."

"Yes, Father." Brand gave a slight bow to both parents and shot his mother a look of gratitude before escaping the room. He knew it was only a matter of time before his father cornered him again, but for now he was free.

NINE

BRAND WAITED WITH Brute approximately fifteen minutes in the clearing before Miss Prudence arrived, toting her puppy by its restraint. Every time he saw her, he was struck anew by her beauty. She wore a burgundy walking dress, a velvet bonnet with matching ribbons, and black gloves. Her dark curls framed her high cheekbones, rosy cheeks, and pert lips. And her eyes—her dark and captivating eyes—contained an impishness about them that made Brand want to smile just looking at her. He didn't want to *stop* looking at her.

With her sister, he had the opposite problem—not because she appeared ghastly by any means. Looking at her simply felt uncomfortable.

"Hello." She smiled cheerfully, revealing her delightful dimple.

Brand nodded and transferred Brute's leash from one hand to the other. "Your suggestion did not work. Your sister's horse was rendered unable to run, and she didn't even fiddle with her bonnet's strings." He sounded like a petulant child, but he didn't care. His father had finally cornered him earlier that morning, and Brand had left the discussion with a renewed determination to put forth his best effort with Miss Gifford.

Miss Prudence didn't reply right away. She allowed her puppy to approach the larger dog, but when Scamp yipped and Brute barked, she crouched down to shush them both. Amazingly enough, they quieted.

She eyed Brute for a long moment before cautiously extending her hand. When he allowed her fingers to graze his head, she smiled. "You are not nearly as frightening as you appear, are you?" She rubbed behind his ears while Scamp sniffed at his feet. Brute directed another bark at the puppy, but Scamp was not so easily cowed. He yipped right back, and the mastiff replied with a snort.

Miss Prudence grinned. "I think you named Scamp well, my lord. I still can't thank you enough."

Brand crouched down to remove Brute's leash. If the beast could not scare away a small puppy, he felt it safe to release him. He cocked his head at Miss Prudence before rising to face her.

"Are you ignoring me on purpose?" In a way, she reminded Brand of her puppy. The top of her head barely reached his shoulders, and her waist couldn't be much larger than the span of his hands, yet she grinned impishly up at him, not the least bit intimidated. It was a stark contrast to her slightly taller sister.

"Why would I ignore you?" she asked.

"Because you are impertinent."

She touched her hand to her heart, as though offended, and leaned closer. "You must have me mistaken for someone else, my lord. I am *not* impertinent. I am prudent—or rather, Prudence."

He chuckled. "I seriously doubt that. Something tells me you take great delight in rebelling against that name."

She conceded his words with a shrug. "I suppose I do. But I am not wholly imprudent either. I prefer to remain somewhere in the middle. What about you, Lord *Knave*? Do you rebel against your name as well, or do you embrace it?"

He caught a whiff of lavender in the air around her. The scent had a wildness and vibrancy to it that suited her. "As with you, I attempt to fall somewhere in the middle. Not a knave but not upstanding either."

"What an interesting pair we make," she said. "Your name is of a wicked nature and mine is decidedly *un*wicked, yet we both find ourselves straying away from them."

"Yes, but I feel the need to point out that I am straying towards a less wicked nature whereas you are doing the opposite."

"What are you implying, my lord?" she asked. "That you are inherently good and I am inherently bad?"

"Only that I am headed in a more virtuous direction."

"Careful, sir, or your pride will puff you up, which will make me the better person in the end."

He chuckled, more than a little interested in the dimple that appeared and disappeared at the edge of her mouth. It looked rather kissable—or perhaps it was *she* who looked kissable.

Brand quickly averted his gaze and retreated a step. "As I was saying," he said, "your brilliant idea to further my acquaintance with your sister did not work."

She tugged on Scamp's leash, pulling the puppy away from a muddy spot, and chided him gently. When at last she glanced back at him, her tone was all innocence. "Did it not? According to Sophia, she felt more like herself with you that morning than ever before."

Brand found that difficult to believe. Perhaps for a moment or two she had peeked out of her hiding place, but like a tortoise feeling threatened, she had been quick to retreat back inside. Was that how it would be if they married? A perpetual game of peek-a-boo?

If so, he would be wise to cease his attentions towards Miss Gifford immediately.

And take them up with whom? Her sister—the one who does not stand to inherit Talford?

Brand kicked at a rock that had been lodged in the dirt, but it didn't budge. Like him, it was trapped. The thought urged him to kick it a bit harder, but the action only served to scuff his boot.

"I can get you a shovel if you'd like," said Miss Prudence playfully. "Or perhaps Scamp or Brute might be compelled to dig it up for you. It is a most interesting rock, is it not? I can see why you are so intent on freeing it. Do you keep a collection of rocks under the floorboards in your room?"

"No, but perhaps I should start. Does Miss Gifford enjoy hunting for rocks? Do you mean to suggest that I invite her on an expedition in the future? I could intentionally forget to bring a pail for the collected pebbles with the hope that she will feel obligated to offer up her bonnet as a replacement. That, of course, will allow me to see the true Miss Gifford at last. Is that your plan?"

Miss Prudence giggled. "You sound addled, my lord. Did you happen to take a fall on your way here this morning?"

He tucked his hands behind his back and squinted up into the trees. "You seem to bring out the ridiculous in me, Miss Prudence. Why else would I agree to answer your many questions? Please tell me you have forgotten about that aspect of our bargain."

"Certainly not." She proceeded to bend down and lift the hem of her dress just enough to remove a pencil and a slip of paper from beneath its folds.

Brand probably should have averted his gaze, but he was far too amused—and curious—to look away. "What have you done, sewn a pocket into your skirt?"

116

Her eyes twinkled in a way that dared him not to be shocked. "My shift, if you must know. How else could I take my pencil and paper to and from the house without detection?"

Brand chuckled at the thought of Miss Prudence sewing a pocket into such a strange location. "Has your laundry maid noticed your handiwork?"

"Yes. She thought it odd until I explained that it would save me from having to carry my reticule when I walk to town. After that, she declared my addition brilliant and even sewed one into her shift as well."

The muscles around Brand's mouth were not used to smiling so much. They started to cramp and protest.

Miss Prudence searched the clearing until her eyes landed on a fallen log. She walked over to it and looped Scamp's restraint around one of the branches before tugging off her gloves and tossing them aside. Her pencil tapped slowly against her lower lip as she skimmed through her notes.

Brand didn't know whether he should feel nervous or intrigued. What had she written on that paper? What questions would come spilling from her mouth? How many of them would he be willing to answer?

After several moments, she lowered the pencil and looked at him. "I should probably begin by telling you that I was moved by Mrs. Harper's tender feelings towards her late husband. She has been my inspiration for this new story, which is why I would like to be introduced to her at some point. You see, I want to write about a love that is fierce and passionate and then . . . lost."

The words "fierce" and "passionate" reverberated through Brand's mind—words an innocent young lady like Miss Prudence probably knew very little about, especially when it came to love. Did she even understand their full meaning? If not, he had no intention of being the one to further her education on the matter.

He cleared his throat. "What became of the story you were writing when I discovered you in the tree?"

She dismissed his question with a wave of her hand. "As I told you before, I have decided to write a more cheerful tale about a love gone right rather than a love gone wrong."

"You consider the loss of a loved one a cheerful tale? Most would call it a tragedy."

She laughed. "It will begin as a tragedy and end on a joyful note. It'll be a tale about healing, overcoming hardship, and discovering it's possible to love again."

In other words, Miss Prudence intended to write not one, but *two* fierce and passionate love stories. Brand slid his fingers beneath the knot of his cravat, loosening it slightly.

"It sounds as though you already have everything worked out," he attempted.

"I do, for the most part," she agreed. "But there are details that I cannot write about because I lack experience and because I am not a man. For example, what does a man notice when he looks upon a woman for the first time? Does he see the intelligence in her eyes? Does he try to get a sense of her character? Does he notice her quiet fortitude or innate stubbornness?"

Brand shuffled his feet and swallowed. He used to believe that he had moved beyond the days when a woman could make him squirm, but apparently not. What would Miss Prudence say if he told her that first thing he noticed about a woman was her beauty—her eyes, her hair, the curves of her body and quality of her skin? Perhaps he'd judge her level of confidence based on her stature, but that would be the extent of his initial observations. Anything beyond that came only after a better acquaintance.

With Miss Gifford, he'd noticed her almost orange hair, her freckles, and the beautiful hue of her wide-set eyes. He'd also noticed her well-defined curves. For all her flaws, Miss Gifford had a very pleasing figure.

But he couldn't very well admit as much to Miss Prudence. Brand wasn't a man who cared much for the opinions of others, with the exception of his parents, Catherine, and a few close friends. But he was coming to care about what Miss Prudence thought of him, and he didn't want her thinking him superficial.

"Perhaps we should begin with a different question," Brand suggested.

The upward curve of her lips indicated that she found his request amusing, although she did not say as much. She merely nodded, attempted to straighten her lips, and perused her list once more. When she lifted her eyes to him again, they sparkled with a challenge.

"I was going to save this question until later so as not to shock you from the get-go, but I really do need to know . . . What does it feel like to kiss a woman?"

A large lump formed in Brand's throat, and his mouth went dry. *What the deuce?* She had promised not to ask questions that would make him uncomfortable, but already he wanted to flee like a frightened kitten. How could he possibly explain how it felt to kiss a woman?

Brand searched his mind for a way to avoid answering until he heard a snicker escape her lips. She was laughing at him. Him! Hildebrand Ethan Cannon, Viscount Knave—a man at least eight years her senior and a great deal higher in social standing.

Unbelievable.

"You are teasing me," he said, hoping it was true. If she'd posed the question to make him squirm—and perhaps make him more inclined to answer her other questions—then she wouldn't be expecting an answer.

She shook her head, still smiling. "I'm afraid not, my lord, although I did find the look of terror on your face vastly amusing."

"I'm glad I could entertain you."

"I hope you will be equally glad to instruct me on a few things as well. The first scene in my book will include a kiss, and I have no idea how to describe the experience. Do a woman's lips feel warm or soft or even moist? Would your pulse quicken? Aside from touch, what other senses are engaged? How would it make you feel and what would you notice when you held a woman in your arms?"

If she thought he'd appeared terror-stricken before, there would be no word for how he looked now. Did she earnestly expect him to answer such questions? Surely even *she* knew how inappropriate it would be to discuss such things, her being an innocent.

"I cannot say," he finally muttered.

Her brow puckered in confusion. "Have you never kissed a woman, my lord?"

Brand was sorely tempted to lie and say he had not, but he couldn't bring himself to do so. Any man of six-and-twenty who had never experienced a kiss would be laughed out of his manhood. Women were expected to remain innocent until married. Men were not.

"Yes, I have kissed a woman," he finally admitted, "but I have no intention of discussing any of the details with you."

"Why not?" she asked, her large brown eyes blinking at him curiously. "Would you rather I invent the information?"

"Yes."

She obviously didn't appreciate his retort because she scowled. "Can you not tell me at least a little?"

"No."

"Why?"

"Because a kiss could never be described with any sort of accuracy, at least not by me. It involves too many feelings and sensations and complexities of thought. If you wish to know what a kiss feels like, you'll have to experience it for yourself."

Too late, Brand realized his mistake. Her expression became contemplative, as though she was actually considering doing just that. Good gads, had he really just encouraged an innocent young woman to go hunting for a kiss? Who would she ask? A groom? Stablehand? The next peddler that came to town?

"I think you are right," she said at last. "I really must experience a kiss for myself if I am to describe it with any sort of accuracy." She blinked up at him with that innocent expression again. "Will *you* kiss me Lord Knave? No, how silly of me. You are to marry my sister, so that would never do." She pursed her lips for a moment before musing, "Perhaps one of the footmen would be kind enough to show me how it's done."

Kind enough? Brand could think of a great many reasons a footman would comply with such a request, and kindness did not factor in to any of them. Brand would kiss her himself before he allowed a footman near her.

He rubbed the bridge of his nose, feeling a headache coming on. "Perhaps I can try to explain what it feels like after all." Better that than having her chase after a footman.

"But you only just said you couldn't do it justice," she pointed out. "I realize I sound dreadfully forward, but I really must know, and experience is the best teacher, is it not?"

"No, it isn't," he lied. "And you are not going to kiss a footman."

"Then who? Felix or Lionel, perhaps? I'm fairly certain I can convince one of them to do it, if given the opportunity. The question is how to go about it?"

It was plain to see by the firm set of her jaw that she would not rest until she had experienced a kiss of her own. She didn't seem to care who did the deed, only that the man did a thorough job of it. A quick peck on the lips wouldn't satisfy her curiosities.

"Perhaps I could send a note to Felix and ask him to call on me," she continued to muse. "We could take a stroll through the maze in the gardens. There is a hidden alcove on the south side, which could be quite perfect. We would have to evade Ruth, obviously, but—"

"Devil take it," Brand growled as he pulled her to him. Her quick intake of breath was the only sound she made before his mouth covered hers. He had planned to make short work of the kiss—just enough to satisfy her—but the moment he felt the softness and warmth of her lips, he forgot all about research and books and lessons. His mouth moved over hers slowly and deliberately. At first, she stood frozen in place with her arms rigid at her side. Then, ever so cautiously, she began to respond, tilting her head a little to the side and matching his movements with some of her own. Eventually, her hands snaked up his chest, and she grabbed hold of his lapels, rising on her tiptoes to increase the pressure of the kiss.

She sighed, and Brand felt any control he still possessed slip away. His hands slid around to the nape of her neck, touching the softness of her hair and skin. How well she fit against him. Her hair smelled of lavender, and her lips tasted like apples and cinnamon. She kissed the way she expressed herself, with honesty, holding nothing back, and Brand had the distinct impression that he was embracing one of the most genuine women he had ever met. The thought wriggled into the crevices of his heart, making him feel something greater than desire.

Devil take it. What was he doing? He grasped her shoulders and pushed her away, keeping her at arms' length as he struggled to regain his composure. What had begun as an education for her had escalated into something it shouldn't have. How had he let that happen?

He looked at her beautiful, flushed face, mussed hair, and sparkling eyes, wanting nothing more than to pull her to him once more. Why couldn't she be the eldest Gifford daughter? Why couldn't she be the heiress of Talford Hall? Why couldn't she be the one he should marry? Brand would have no trouble courting her. In fact, he would look forward to it.

Curse his wretched luck.

She drew in a shaky breath and stared at him for what felt like an eternity. Her eyes were round balls of darkness, peering at him in confusion and wonder.

At last she managed a tenuous smile. "I suppose I needn't escape to the gardens with Felix any longer."

"No. I suppose not." Brand turned away, cursing inwardly. That kiss would be forever ingrained in his memory. How could he possibly go back to courting her sister after this?

"I can see now why you did not think you could adequately describe the sensation. It was quite . . . well, sensational, wasn't it? Is that the way it always feels? I had expected it would be a pleasurable experience, but I had no notion it would feel so . . ." Her hands flew to her rosy cheeks. "Goodness, I can see now why men and women are so fond of kissing."

She was making it deucedly difficult not to kiss her

again. Brand wanted to tell her that not all kisses felt that sensational. Very few did, in fact. His lips still burned from the touch, and his heartbeat had yet to slow.

"I must thank you, Lord Knave, for answering my question so . . . well."

Brand nearly answered, "It was my pleasure," before he thought better of it. Although it *had* been a pleasure, he could never admit that to her. Let her think the kiss had been nothing more than an answer to a question and that all embraces felt that way. One day she would learn otherwise, but with any luck, the memory of their kiss would have faded by then. He could only pray it would eventually fade for him.

She crouched down to collect her pencil and paper, which she'd apparently dropped at some point, then walked over to take a seat on the log. She played with Scamp for a moment or two before lifting her gaze to his.

Her voice was a mixture of timid and hopeful when she asked, "Shall we return to my first question now?"

Her first question? Brand had to wonder if the kiss had affected her as much as it had him. A pink hue still stained her cheeks, but other than that, she seemed to have recovered from their embrace. For the life of him, he couldn't recall what that first question had been, only that he hadn't wanted to answer it.

"Have you forgotten already?" she asked, correctly interpreting his expression. "Or are you simply hoping that *I* had forgotten?"

Brand looked away, thinking a dip in a cool pond might clear his head. "Perhaps we should continue this conversation another time."

"No, please," she begged. "If I am to make any progress at all beyond the first few chapters of my story, I must know what a man first notices about a woman. I realize I am asking a great deal of you, Lord Knave, but you are the only person I dare ask. Please do not desert me."

Brand felt like he was being given a taste of the power his mother wielded over his father. Oddly enough, he found himself wanting to capitulate even though he knew it was a bad idea. He should leave at once and stay as far away from Miss Prudence as humanly possible.

Instead, he leaned his shoulder against the trunk of the tree and mustered an unaffected tone. Perhaps if he turned the tables on her, she would cease her pestering. "Tell me, Miss Prudence, what is it that *you* first notice about a man?"

The question didn't seem to discomfit her at all. She pursed her lips in thought, tapping her pencil against her lower lip as she'd done before. After a moment, she lowered it to her lap and shrugged. "I suppose I first notice a man's appearance—what he looks like and whether or not he is handsome. After that, I noticed how he carries himself. Is it with confidence or arrogance? Does he seem timid or skittish? Do his eyes have an intelligent look about them? Does he smile often, and is it a nice smile? Does he appear kind or critical? Is he someone I would wish to meet or do my best to avoid?"

Brand could only stare at her. He didn't know what he'd expected her to say, but not that. It made him feel both shallow and unobservant. "You can detect all of that on first glance?"

"No. But I do look for those things, especially if the man is of interest to me. If I understand something about his nature first, it is easier to know how to speak with him should we meet. With some men, I can tell straightaway that my forthright ways will not shock them. Others, I am more cautious around, like Mr. Winston. One look was all it took to recognize that he was a serious-minded man who would not tolerate teasing. And he doesn't—tolerate teasing, that is. Or speaking, for that matter."

"In other words," said Brand, "you form instant judgments of people."

She nodded, not appearing the least bit abashed by her admission. "I prefer to think of them as conclusions. But don't we all conclude things about each other in some way? I'm not saying I am always correct or that my mind cannot be changed. Some men have surprised me most pleasantly, yourself included."

Brand dusted a few bark shavings from the sleeve of his coat before meeting her gaze. "I was the rake who met a woman in the library to arrange a lover's tryst."

She smiled a little. "Yes, but my low opinion of you started long before that."

His eyes widened slightly. Was she in earnest? What could she have possibly found to despise in him? "Did you think me hideous?" he asked. "Arrogant? Sadly lacking in intelligence?"

She shifted positions slightly and leaned forward, resting her elbows on her knees. "Naturally, I did not think you hideous—you are far too handsome for that. While you may have struck me as a little arrogant, you appeared more confident than proud and definitely had a look of intelligence about you. In truth, what I found lacking in you was your character."

He didn't know whether to be amused or affronted by her candid assessment. "A man of low character from just one look?"

"It wasn't only one look, my lord. You are to marry my sister, so I paid more attention to you than I would have otherwise done, and . . . well, you appeared to have a wandering eye."

Nothing she could've said would have surprised Brand more. A wandering eye? However did she form that conclusion?

She must have noticed the disbelief in his expression because she clarified, "I often saw your gaze travel in the direction of Mrs. Harper. The two of you exchanged several glances that appeared more flirtatious than friendly, and I didn't know what else to think but the worst."

Brand thought back to that evening. He and Catherine had been good friends for years, and he could see how someone might misinterpret their glances, especially someone as observant as Miss Prudence. Even his mother had remarked on the possibility of Brand developing feelings for Catherine. How many others present had thought the same?

Brand sauntered over to where Miss Prudence sat on the log and sank down next to her. A short stub of a branch knot dug into his backside, so he shifted closer to her, his arm brushing against hers. He became keenly aware of her proximity but couldn't bring himself to move away.

"Before that night," he explained, "it had been a year since I had seen Catherine. The last time I laid eyes on her, she had been dressed in black. Her eyes were red and swollen and contained a haunted, miserable look about them, and I wondered if I would ever see her smile again. So when I spied her across the ballroom, dressed in blue and looking almost like her old, vibrant self, I couldn't help but seek her out. The joy in her expression was a wonderful sight to behold." Indeed, it had been a balm to the guilt he had been shouldering for so long, allowing Brand to feel a measure of hope. How long had it been since he had felt that?

A soft smile touched Miss Prudence's lips, and a newfound respect shown in her eyes. "I suspected that was your reason, but it is good to hear you say so. I certainly did form the wrong conclusions about you in the beginning, didn't I? Forgive me?"

"Conclusion*s*?" he asked, emphasizing the plural form of the word. "Never say you found more in me to dislike."

She waved her hand flippantly. "Nothing of consequence. I merely assumed you were a bore."

A bore? "You cannot be serious."

"Indeed I am." Her voice had a wistful quality to it, as though she was more bothered by the fact that she had been mistaken than wrongly accusing him.

"But we didn't exchange more than a few words with each other," he pointed out. "How could you possibly have come by that opinion?"

"Oh, it had nothing to do with your behavior that night. I made that assumption from something my sister said."

"Your *sister* thinks I'm a bore?" If anyone could be described as such, it was Miss Gifford. Brand, at least, *attempted* to make lively conversation.

"No, Sophia does not think that—nor would she say if she did. She only mentioned that you rarely strayed beyond discussions about the weather or the graciousness of your hosts." She turned to examine him. "Honestly, my lord, the weather? Could you think of nothing else to say? Now that I know you better, I find myself most surprised."

Brand leaned back and glanced at the skies through the trees above. "Is it not a fine day today, Miss Prudence?" he said dryly. "Have you ever beheld a more glorious blue in the sky?"

She slapped his knee in a playful manner. "Do stop, sir. You know very well that we have more interesting things to discuss than the color of the sky."

"Yes, well, unfortunately, your sister and I rarely do. The fact that we were able to converse about the weather for a time was a miracle."

She didn't answer right away. She only watched him, pursing her lips in that way he was coming to like far too much. How simple it would be to lean over and kiss her. Would she be shocked if he did? Would she believe him if he told her that kisses felt different while sitting and she needed to experience it from that perspective as well?

Brand pried his eyes away and focused on the antics of Scamp, who was currently following a beetle with his nose. Not far away, Brute lounged under the shade of a tree.

"I have it," Miss Prudence said suddenly, placing her hand on his knee. As before, her touch had an instantaneous effect, wearing down his barely-veiled control.

"You have invited Sophia to dine with you at Radbourne tomorrow evening, haven't you?"

"My parents have invited your entire family—*you* included."

She waved off his last words. "I will most likely not be there, but Sophia will, and after dinner you must invite her for a walk through the gardens with Brute."

"Brute?"

"Yes." She nodded, appearing excited. "Sophia has always had an affinity with animals, though she will never admit it is anything out of the ordinary. But she is wrong. She's quite brilliant with them and has never come across a creature that doesn't warm to her instantly—with the exception of reptiles and rodents and insects, obviously, although a butterfly landed on her finger only last week. Anyway, she is a wonder with horses, dogs, cats, and the like. You should explain to her the problems you are experiencing with Brute, and I'll wager my entire stash of pencils she'll have a great many things to say on the subject. Not only that, but she will probably provide you with some valuable help where he is concerned."

Brand refrained from telling her that Brute had already shown marked improvement, which he attributed mostly to her and Scamp. Still, he rubbed his knuckles across his lower lip as though considering her idea even though the thought of accompanying Miss Gifford on a walk through the gardens didn't appeal to him in the least. Accompanying her younger sister, however, appealed far more than it should.

"Is there a reason you won't be joining us at Radbourne on Friday?" he asked.

After all they had discussed—and experienced—Brand never would have imagined that such an innocent question could unsettle her. But that's exactly how she appeared. Unsettled and ill at ease.

"I, er . . . well, I am not officially out yet, and . . ." Her voice trailed off, and she focused her gaze on a small patch of grass near her feet.

"And . . ." he prodded, wanting her to continue.

She pressed down on the grass with her slipper. "It's simple, really. My mother feels as though Sophia should have her time in society first, which is perfectly understandable. My time will come later."

"But you attended Mrs. Hilliard's dance."

"Only because Mother accepted the invitation before she knew—" Her voice stopped abruptly, and her cheeks became quite red. Unlike her sister, the sight was most becoming on her.

Brand leaned near her, pressing his shoulder into hers. "Come now, Miss Prudence. Do not turn prudent on me now."

She worried over her lower lip a moment more taking a deep breath and blowing it out the side of her mouth in an expression of defeat. "Very well. If you must know, Mother granted me permission to attend the dance before she knew that you would be in attendance. As I am the more . . . outgoing of her daughters, she worries that I will draw too much attention away from Sophia. I never mean to do it, you realize, but . . ."

"It happens?" he finished for her, knowing the truth of it from his own experience.

She shrugged. "I suppose on occasion, but certainly not to the extent or in the way my mother thinks. In the eyes of most men, I am nothing more than an incorrigible child. How could I possibly pose any threat to Sophia? Not only is she beautiful, but she is poised and refined in a way that I can never hope to be."

If Miss Prudence thought men viewed her that way, she thought wrong. The night of the dance, she had garnered the attention of most every man in the room, and the looks they gave her were certainly not the looks of doting big brothers. She was only fooling herself if she thought men viewed her as a child. Brand certainly didn't.

"Does Sophia feel the same as your mother?" he asked. "Would she prefer that you remain at home as well?"

She shook her head. "Sophia is too kind-hearted to ever want that, and I think my presence makes her feel a bit more comfortable in society. She can be herself with me, you see, and it relieves her mind to know that I will fill in the gap if she's ever at a shortage for words."

Not for the first time Brand wondered what the eldest Gifford daughter was truly like. Did she have a sense of humor buried inside her somewhere? Did he have any hope of breaking through her shell if he exercised more patience? Did he even want to any longer?

When it came down to it, that was the crux of the problem. He didn't. The more he pursued her, the less he wanted to make another attempt at it. A responsible and dutiful son would do whatever it took to align both families, but how could he advance his courtship with Miss Gifford when the memory of holding and kissing her sister would forever be emblazoned on his mind? It was Miss Prudence he wanted to court, not Miss Gifford.

Despite all this, Brand couldn't give up on the eldest daughter just yet. It felt unfair to do so when, according to his mother and her sister, he didn't know her. Perhaps she *would* pleasantly surprise him.

It was a hope he needed to cling to for the sake of his family.

"I think," Brand forced himself to say, "that a stroll in the garden with your sister and Brute will be just the thing." The words fell flat, but Miss Prudence didn't seem to notice. A beautiful smile crinkled the corners of her eyes and revealed her adorable dimple, making Brand want to kiss her all over again.

Blast. Blast. Blast.

He dragged his body up from the log and whistled for Brute, knowing he needed to leave before he did something he'd likely regret. He had been a fool to suggest this meeting in the woods, and now it was time to retreat and regroup. He should be grateful Miss Prudence would not be coming to dinner with her family. Perhaps then he would be able to give her sister the attention she deserved.

"You're leaving?" she asked, holding fast to her paper and pencil as she scrambled to her feet.

Brand nodded, looking away. "I'm afraid I must."

"Can you at least answer my question before you go?"

Brute, the wretched dog that he was, had disregarded the whistle and continued to lounge in the shade of the tree. Losing patience with himself, the dog, and the entire sticky situation, Brand turned around and found Miss Prudence standing directly behind him, close enough for him to see the flecks of gold in her eyes.

Throwing caution to the wind, he said, "When I first looked upon you, I noticed the darkness of your eyes, the luster and color of your hair, your beautiful eyebrows, high cheekbones, and perfectly shaped lips. I noticed the way you walked and danced, caught the impertinent sparkle in your eyes, and delighted in the sound of your laughter. You see, I, unlike you, did not form any opinions about your intelligence or personality or level of goodness. I merely noticed a beautiful woman."

As he spoke, her eyes grew wide, and she took a step back, appearing almost fearful. "I didn't ask for your opinion of *me*," she breathed.

Brand wanted to curse and retract his too-hasty words in an instant. What had he been thinking to say such things, especially now that he knew her fears concerning her sister? Did he want her to worry that she was in danger of stealing away her sister's so-called intended?

No. He didn't. That should be *his* concern to shoulder, not hers. Miss Prudence might be at liberty to speak her true thoughts concerning him, but he was certainly not at liberty to do the same.

He sighed and turned away. "I noticed many beautiful women that night, Miss Prudence. I noticed eyes, hair, complexions, gowns, and figures. Does that shock you? Do you now think me the shallowest of men?"

She didn't answer.

"The fact of the matter is that I *am* a man, and as such I tend to see the outside of a person first. The inside comes later, only after a longer acquaintance."

Silence met his words, and Brand could only wonder at what she could be thinking. He peeked back at her, noting the menagerie of emotions in her expression. Confusion, worry, surprise—perhaps even some disappointment. He couldn't tell for certain, and he refused to ask because he should not care.

Instead, he held out his hand. "Why not give me that paper, and I shall take it with me and write my answers down for you? In a few days' time, I will return to this spot and tuck it into that hole in the log where you can retrieve it at your leisure. How does that sound?"

She nodded slowly but continued to clutch the paper, as though she did not like his plan but knew it was for the best. Or perhaps she had changed her mind and no longer wanted him to answer her questions. Whatever the reason for her reticence, Brand didn't care for the plan either. He didn't want to return to this place, leave a note in a log, and slink away without seeing her. He wanted to meet with her again, speak to her, kiss her, enjoy her smiles and laughter and teasing, and look into those beautiful dark eyes. He wanted to walk up the steps at Talford Hall and ask to take *her* for a ride instead of her sister.

Unfortunately, he was not at liberty to do any of those things.

At long last, she held out the paper, but snatched it back as soon as he reached for it. "I will give you this only if you promise to answer all of the questions truthfully, even if they make you sound like the shallowest of men. Agreed?"

Brand found himself charmed all over again. "Agreed."

He accepted the page and tucked it into his coat pocket before whistling for Brute once more, but the obstinate beast didn't budge.

Miss Prudence tilted her head to the side and smiled sadly. "I shall miss our visits, my lord. You are the only one who knows my secret, and I suddenly feel as though I am losing my one and only confidant. But at the same time, I understand."

The words touched Brand's heart. Why couldn't more women be as open and honest as Miss Prudence? He would miss that about her. He'd miss a great many things. "Perhaps I am not the only one guilty of giving your sister less credit than she deserves. Why not make *her* your confidant?"

Prudence seemed to consider his words for a moment before shaking her head. "I dare not. If I ever lost her good opinion—if she even attempted to talk me out of writing stories as my mother would do—I couldn't bear it. You heard her when you encountered me on the road and you inquired about that page you found. She insisted that her sister would never write such nonsense. If she ever found out that I was the one who wrote that page . . . well, she would lose all respect for me."

"Or maybe she would respect you more," Brand said, wondering, not for the first time, what it would be like to have a brother. Once upon a time, his parents had wanted more children but those children had never come, and the only person who had ever come close to filling the shoes of a brother died a year prior.

"I will consider it," said Miss Prudence. "In the meantime, thank you for your help and for not making me feel as though I'm wrong—or mad—for wanting to write stories."

"I *do* think you're mad," teased Brand. "No sane woman would climb a tree to eavesdrop on a clandestine meeting."

She laughed quietly. "Well then, thank you for not attempting to talk me out of writing."

"Somehow, I knew it would be a fruitless effort. And besides, from what I read before, you seem to have a talent for it."

Her smile widened, and Brand knew he needed to leave.

"I really must go." He turned and whistled again. "Brute, here boy!"

Only after Scamp yipped did Brute finally decide to obey. Brand strode forward to meet the wretched dog, and without looking back, said, "Good day, Miss Prudence."

"Good day, my lord."

TEN

PRUDENCE FELT UNACCOUNTABLY irritable during her walk back to Talford Hall. She tugged on Scamp's restraint, keeping him from inspecting a mound of dirt. He tried to resist, but his little body was not strong enough to do battle with Prudence's current mood.

"Come, Scamp. We've spent far too long in the woods, and it is past time for us to return home. Mother and Sophia will be wondering what has become of us."

Scamp yipped in response but followed nonetheless.

As soon as the side of Talford Hall came into view, with its ivy-clad stone walls, Scamp must have realized his freedom was about to come to an end because he attempted to dart back into the woods. He only got as far as his leash would allow before he protested by yipping and whining. Prudence looked down at her forlorn puppy, and her heart softened a little.

"Yes, I know you do not want to say goodbye to our new friends and go inside, but even you must realize it is for the best. Lord Knave is to marry my sister, and Brute does not belong to him. If we become too attached, it'll be to our detriment. Don't you see?"

Even though Prudence knew Scamp did not see at all— or likely even care—it made her feel stronger and wiser to take on the role of teacher. She preferred giving lectures to receiving them, even though her words were more for her benefit than the puppy's.

Lord Knave had been right to insist on taking his leave, and Prudence had been wrong to beg him for answers to her questions. Even now, the memory of his lips against hers and his hands in her hair sent shivers through her entire body. She had asked him if every kiss felt as blissful, but deep down, she knew that could not be the case. Mr. Winston could never transport her to such an exquisite realm. Prudence had felt the passion, complexity of thoughts, and all the sensations Lord Knave had said he could never describe, and oh, what a lesson.

But had it been merely a lesson? For a few moments, Prudence had thought it had, at least for Lord Knave. It had been the hope she'd clung to, the thing that enabled her to pretend it had been nothing more than a lesson for her as well. But then she had to beg for another answer to another question. Why had she done that? Why hadn't she left well enough alone?

Even now, the honesty of his words thudded around in her head, pleasing and unnerving her all over again. She had been so certain that he viewed her only as a silly child, but after he had kissed her in that way, looked at her with such intensity, and called her beautiful, she realized that she had been wrong about him yet again.

Yes, he'd confessed to assessing many other women that night, but why had he chosen Prudence as the example and not Sophia? If he should have praised anyone's beauty, it should have been the woman he intended to marry, not her younger sister. It felt wrong and right at the same time, which bothered Prudence the most. It shouldn't have felt right at all.

The entire exchange settled like a heavy stone in her stomach, one that Prudence couldn't be rid of. The fact that she had enjoyed her time with Lord Knave immensely did not help matters at all. Had he kissed her with such passion to teach her how it feels, or had he become lost to it as well? Something told her it was the latter. Before today, she had thought her attraction to him one-sided—a childlike fascination that she'd eventually outgrow—but now . . . well, now she did not know what to think. Had she inadvertently placed herself between him and her sister?

She pressed her palm into her stomach in an attempt to calm the ever-rising sickness. What sort of person would do such a thing?

Prudence suddenly pictured herself as a villain in a nefarious plot, pretending to be good and kind and have the best interests of her loved ones at heart. But really she was nothing more than a thieving, duplicitous traitor who deserved to be tossed into a dungeon.

Prudence shivered at the thought, desperately wanting to go back to the time when she'd considered Lord Knave to be a womanizing bore. Why couldn't he have been that person? Why did he have to be charming and likable and wonderful? At the very least, why couldn't he have looked down on her for wanting to write books or taken her to task the way her mother would have? If he had, Prudence wouldn't have met him in the woods, she wouldn't have offered to help him woo her sister, and he wouldn't have agreed to answer her questions regarding her story. They would never have kissed, and she would not be experiencing such turmoil now.

Oh, what a jumbled up mess of her own creation.

Prudence could only be grateful that her mother intended to keep her out of the social scene for now. Perhaps if she ceased speaking to Lord Knave and encountering him in the woods, she would come to forget all about this afternoon.

She *had* to forget if he was to be her brother-in-law.

Prudence dragged Scamp around the side of the house and paused when she spotted a familiar gig out front. She wanted to cry out for joy at the blessed sight. Abby had come. If there was ever a time Prudence needed a distraction, it was now. She scooped up her obstinate puppy and quickened her steps towards the house.

As soon as she walked into the great hall, Sophia's voice called from the parlor, "Pru, is that you? Look who has come for a visit."

Prudence strode into the parlor and attempted to smile at her friend, who looked like sunshine itself. Abby's afternoon dress was an almost startling shade of yellow, and along with her matching bonnet, golden hair, and light blue eyes, she presented a most cheerful sight.

"It is about time you came to call," said Prudence, striving to sound as though nothing was amiss. "I was beginning to think of you as more a stranger than a friend."

Abby reached out to rub Scamp's head. "The road can be traveled in both directions, you know. And who is this little darling? I don't believe I have ever seen anything so precious."

"This scamp of a creature is called Scamp, obviously."

Abby laughed, taking the puppy from Prudence's arms and cradling him in her own. "You are far too sweet to be named Scamp. What were you thinking to call him such a thing? Cuddles would have been much more appropriate."

Prudence grimaced, not liking the name at all, though perhaps she should consider calling him something different. Otherwise, every time she called out "Scamp," she would probably think of Lord Knave and how wonderful it had been to speak with him and laugh with him and be held by him.

Prudence glanced at her sister, and a fresh bout of guilt washed over her.

Unfortunately, Scamp's name suited him too perfectly to ever think of him as anything else.

"I can see now why you have not visited me," said Abby as she tucked Scamp close to her bosom. "But I will not excuse you after today. I expect to see you both at Chillhorne in the not-so-distant future, and you must bring Cuddles as well."

"Scamp," Prudence corrected. "His name is Scamp."

"To you, perhaps, but not to me."

Prudence exchanged a smile with Sophia before sitting on the chair beside her friend. "You now understand why I have been a stranger of late, but what about you, Abby? Have you acquired a new puppy as well?"

"I only wish," said Abby. "With Papa gone away on business much of the time, I would dearly love a puppy to distract me."

"You are always welcome here, you know," said Prudence. "I wish you'd feel comfortable staying with us while your father is away. We would have such fun, the three of us."

Abby combed her fingers through Scamp's soft fur, looking perfectly content. "I *would* feel comfortable here, but Papa is never gone for more than a day or two."

"Yes, only to leave again straightaway," said Prudence.

Abby smiled sadly. "I am well aware of his business habits. But I prefer to be at home when he comes and goes. That is the only way I know how to stay connected, not that we are close by any means. But we are better than we would be if I made myself scarce." Abby's mother had died giving birth to her, and although she would never say as much, Prudence knew her friend missed the mother she never had and the father who was always too preoccupied with business. Her Great-aunt Josephine, who acted as her companion, accompanied Abby to social events when her father was out of town, but that was the extent of her companionship. The older woman preferred the comforts of Chillhorne and probably slept more than she roused. Abby usually brought her maid with her to Talford.

"You haven't said what has kept you away," Prudence reminded her.

A blush stole across Abby's cheeks. "Let us just say that Chillhorne House has not been nearly as lonely of late."

Intrigued, Prudence waited for more, but when no more came, she glanced instead at her sister for answers. Sophia shrugged, obviously as clueless as Prudence.

"Could you be any more cryptic, Abby?" Prudence asked.

Abby laughed. "Yes, and I am very tempted to keep you in suspense, but that would be unkind of me, so I will refrain. The fact of the matter is that I have found a new friend at Chillhorne. His name is William Penroth. He is the nephew of our new steward, recently come from school to apprentice with his uncle."

This was news to Prudence, especially considering that Abby had always frowned on associations with the lower classes. But now she seemed downright smitten. With the *steward's nephew.*

Prudence had to fight to keep her smile at bay. "Am I to assume Mr. Penroth is handsome?" she asked.

"Handsome, intelligent, kind, and charming. In a way he has become the brother I never had."

Prudence looked at Sophia again, which was the wrong thing to do. Her sister's quirking lips nearly made Prudence laugh out loud.

"Honestly, Abby," said Prudence, doing her best not to smile. "A brother? I'm afraid that blush on your cheeks belies your words. Admit it. Your feelings are not at all sisterly."

Abby laughed. "Perhaps not, but I know better than to fall in love with an apprentice to a land steward. I would never consider engaging in anything more than a harmless flirtation, which is all it is. But I now look forward to the start of each new day, which is something I never could have said before. I can talk to William about anything, and for the first time since Great-aunt Josephine replaced my governess, I have not felt alone in my own house. It has been a blessed change."

"What does your aunt think of your new friend?" Sophia asked.

Abby combed her fingers through Scamp's fur and shrugged. "She doesn't have much to say on the subject, considering she spends much of her time snoozing in her favorite chair and has no notion our steward even has a nephew."

Sophia's smile became wistful. "I am glad to hear you have found such a friend at Chillhorne, Abby. You make me wish I could say the same of Lord Knave."

Prudence startled at the sound of his name and quickly chided herself for overreacting to it. What had her sister meant by that anyway? "Are you in earnest, Sophia? I thought you could be content with any man so long as he offered you wealth and a title."

"I believe Pru's romantic notions are at last having an effect on you, Sophia," teased Abby.

Sophia immediately shook her head, looking slightly embarrassed. "I really don't know why I said that."

Abby rose, taking Scamp with her, and walked over to sit beside Sophia. She encouraged the puppy to jump from her lap to Sophia's, and almost immediately, Sophia smiled.

"Hello, Scamp," she said, mussing the puppy's hair. "I have missed you today."

Abby fiddled with the lace on her gloves before speaking. "I know what loneliness feels like, Sophia. I have lived with it for a great many years, and I wouldn't wish it on anyone. We may tease Pru about her fanciful views on romance, but it is not wrong to want more from a marriage than comforts and status. If there is one thing that William has taught me, it's that I would very much like to marry a man I can call my friend. If he also happens to be handsome and charming, so much the better."

"I'm certain you will find such a man," said Sophia carefully. "Unfortunately, I don't have much choice in the matter of who I marry. I should be grateful it is a man like Lord Knave and not a bounder or a cad."

"But you *do* have a choice," insisted Prudence, more than a little bothered that her sister felt that way. "We *all* have a choice."

Sophia gave her sister a look that suggested Prudence had no idea what she was talking about. "Would you have me defy Mama and look elsewhere for a suitor, Pru? Would you have me spurn the most sought-after man in Oxfordshire with the hope that I will find someone more to my liking? And if I ever did find such a man, what are the odds that he would take a second look in my direction? Lord Knave is courting me only because I am heiress to our family's estate, not because he wishes to make me his wife."

Prudence glared at her sister, tired of hearing Sophia demean herself. "You must stop speaking like that, Sophia. You make it sound as though you are hideous when you are nothing of the sort. You have red hair and a few freckles, that is all. You are not disfigured or repulsive. And I am not suggesting that you spurn Lord Knave. He is a good and honorable man who will make you a fine husband. But you must stop withholding your true self from him and allow him to see you as you are."

As soon as Prudence had spoken the words, she knew she shouldn't have said them—at least not all of them. Curse her quick temper and unruly tongue. It had gotten her into trouble on more than one occasion, and from the looks Abby and Sophia directed at her, she was in trouble again. No one knew about her friendship with Lord Knave, and she didn't intend for them to know either. Like her stories, she had planned to hide that knowledge away where no one but her and Lord Knave would ever know of it.

"I thought you did not care for Lord Knave," said Sophia carefully.

Goodness, how was Prudence to explain her way out of this one? The only known encounters she'd had with the man had been their brief meeting at the dance and their exchange on the roadside. Could she claim a change of heart from those two instances?

"I only think that I may have misjudged him," she hedged.

"What makes you say that?" asked Abby.

Prudence drew her lower lip into her mouth while two pairs of eyes stared at her, waiting for a believable answer. If there was ever a time that she wished for an interruption from her mother or father, now was that time. She would even be grateful for an impromptu visit from Mr. Winston.

In that moment, Lord Knave's words entered her mind. *Perhaps you and I are both guilty of giving your sister less credit than she deserves. Why not make her your confidant?*

She glanced at her sister, weighing out her possible reaction. How much easier it was to give advice than to take it. Did she dare tell Sophia that she had encountered Lord Knave in the woods? Would she think Prudence deceitful and improper and conniving?

Prudence swallowed and forced the words out. "Scamp and I happened upon Lord Knave a time or two during our walks in the woods, and I have been able to get to know him a little better." Sophia didn't need to know about the tree incident. Or the kiss. Or the fact that Lord Knave thought Prudence beautiful. Nor did she need to know that only their first encounter had been by chance.

The word "confidant" didn't necessarily mean that one must confide everything, did it?

Prudence had to push aside her guilt before continuing. "He was walking Mrs. Harper's mastiff, you see, hoping to calm the unruly beast. Brute can be intimidating when he wishes to be and caused me quite a fright at first." Goodness, why had she said that? She was rambling and fidgeting and behaving like a ninnyhammer.

She breathed in deeply and closed her eyes for a moment, trying to calm herself. She couldn't undo what she had done, but that did not mean she couldn't continue to encourage a match between Lord Knave and her sister. In fact, that was precisely what she *should* do. It was the right thing, the honorable thing.

She opened her eyes and searched her sister's face. "He asked about you, Soph. He wished to know how he could come to know you better. Please don't despise me, but I was the one who suggested he take you riding. Only you didn't remove your bonnet, and—"

"You told him about that?" Sophia gasped, her humiliation obvious.

"How could I not? It is part of who you are, Soph, and believe it or not, Lord Knave wasn't the least bit appalled. In fact, he thought it charming and genuinely looked forward to seeing that side of you. Only you didn't show it to him, did you?"

Sophia looked away, her expression troubled and conflicted.

Prudence sighed and softened her tone. "He doesn't have a condemning nature, nor will he think less of you if you remove your bonnet and let your hair come loose. Like you, he is a good person who is trying to do the right thing by his family."

Silence fell upon the room like a heavy quilt, stifling Prudence and making her believe she had been wrong to confide in her sister. She should have come up with another excuse or fibbed or pled a headache, not that anyone would have believed that. Instead, she had listened to Lord Knave's voice in her head, allowing him to sway her into revealing a portion of her carefully guarded secrets. It had been a mistake.

Abby was the first to speak. She clasped her hands to her chest and pasted on a smile. "I suddenly find myself quite parched. Would it be unforgivable of me to request that we send for some tea?"

"Oh dear, I neglected to do that, didn't I?" Sophia handed the puppy back to Abby and jumped up to ring the bell. A moment later, the butler agreed to send a maid for a tray directly.

"I had planned to ring for it when Abby first arrived, but we decided to wait for you, Pru. I'm afraid your arrival drove it from my mind. I'm sorry, Abby."

"I don't mind in the least," said Abby good-naturedly.

Sophia settled back on the sofa, and Prudence watched her closely, looking for signs of distress or frustration. Her sister had every right to be upset with her, but she didn't look anxious or happy or anything else. She appeared the way she usually did—composed and unruffled.

"Soph, if I said anything out of turn, I apologize. I meant you no harm. I only wish to see you happy."

Sophia's expression softened. "I know you didn't, Pru. That thought never even crossed my mind."

"You're not upset with me then?"

"How could I be? Only the dearest of sisters would look out for me in such a way. If I am troubled by anything, it is the concern that I won't be able to get over my reticence with Lord Knave. But I shall make a renewed effort to try, beginning with tomorrow at dinner. Which reminds me. I have had a talk with Mother, and she has agreed to let you accompany us."

Prudence attempted to appear pleased by the news even though it caused her stomach to twist and turn. "Indeed?"

"I pointed out that the invitation was addressed to our entire family, and it would reflect poorly on us to leave my sister behind." Sophia leaned forward. "Do say you will come, Pru. I *need* you to come."

Prudence glanced at Abby before blurting, "It would be better if I didn't. My presence will upset the balance and make the numbers uneven. And you do not need me, Soph. What you *need* to do is learn to converse with Lord Knave on your own. Once you are married, it will only be the two of you. I will not be removing to Radbourne Abbey as you well know. That would be absurd." *And horrible*, she added to herself, cringing inwardly at the thought of seeing Lord Knave every day, the husband of her sister.

"Yes, I understand that," said Sophia, "and I *will* try to be myself from this point forward. Just promise you will come with us tomorrow. That is all I ask of you."

Prudence couldn't promise anything of the sort. Her presence would only get in the way, and she had no desire to observe Lord Knave attempt to woo her sister. But she couldn't bring herself to say no either, not with Sophia imploring her in such a way.

"Very well," Prudence managed.

"Thank you." The warmth in her sister's gaze only worsened the guilt pulling on her insides. Prudence may have agreed to go to the dinner, but come tomorrow afternoon, she had every intention of feigning a stomach ailment. As wrong as it was to go back on her word, she finally understood her mother's concerns about Sophia and even agreed with them.

It would be far better for Sophia if Prudence remained behind.

ELEVEN

"WOULD YOU CARE to go for a stroll with me in the gardens, Miss Gifford?" Brand asked, not sure whether or not he wanted her to accept. She'd spoken hardly a word during dinner. The only reason it had not been an awkward affair was because both sets of parents had a great deal to say to one another. It was made very clear that they were good friends and Lord Knave and Miss Gifford were not.

When Sophia did not answer right away, Mrs. Gifford took it upon herself to speak for her daughter. "She would love to take a stroll with you, my lord. It is a beautiful evening, dearest, and I know how you love walking through the gardens at Talford."

She nodded graciously and rose to retrieve her wrap, but she looked panicked, as though he had asked her to perform on stage in front of a large gathering. Was he that frightening? Her younger sister didn't seem to think so.

Brand turned back to the others. "Would anyone care to join us?"

His mother waved him away. "Perhaps another time, dearest. The four of us monopolized the conversation quite rudely during dinner, and I'm certain you would like an opportunity to converse with Miss Gifford on your own for a time."

"Yes," he agreed. "I have heard she has an affinity for animals, so I thought I would introduce her to Brute. He can serve as our chaperone."

His mother's eyes widened, and she gave him a look that said, *Please tell me you are joking.* "Oh, I'm sure Miss Gifford has no wish to meet that unruly beast, Hildebrand. Why not simply enjoy the beautiful evening?"

"Actually, Lady Bradden," said Sophia, "I would love to meet—Brute, is it? I enjoy all animals, unruly or not. In fact, the unrulier the better."

This comment garnered the surprise of everyone in the room, including Brand.

"Is that a fact?" asked Lord Bradden.

"Indeed," she insisted. "I cannot boast many talents, but I have always loved animals no matter their temperaments."

Brand couldn't have been more pleased by Miss Gifford's show of pluck. He never would have thought her capable of speaking her mind so directly if he hadn't observed it himself. He hoped she would continue.

Perhaps Miss Prudence had been right in suggesting a stroll with Brute after all. If she were here now, he would undoubtedly see a gleam of triumph in those dark brown eyes.

Brand shook his head to clear his mind of her and held an arm out for Miss Gifford. "Let us fetch Brute, shall we?"

"With pleasure," she said.

It didn't take long for Brand to see that Miss Gifford's claims were not unfounded. The moment Brute bounded out of the stables, barking as he barreled towards them, Miss Gifford's smile became more genuine than he had ever seen. In fact, she appeared quite stunning.

She crouched down to meet the dog at eye level, showing no sign of fear, and gave his head a hearty rub, laughing when the animal turned to lick her face.

"He doesn't seem the least bit unruly to me," she said. "He's quite sweet."

"Yes, well he isn't normally this friendly with strangers—or anyone really. Only the other day, when we encountered a stranger during our walk, he growled and barked something fierce."

She gave Brute one last rub and stood. "I don't believe it."

"I can hardly believe it myself anymore, but 'tis true. After Stephen's passing, Brute stopped minding Catherine completely and became something of a beast. She couldn't manage him and even contemplated finding him a new home. I knew it would be difficult for her to lose one more thing, so I talked her into letting me have a go at retraining him."

Miss Gifford nodded. "It makes sense. Dogs probably do not understand loss the way we do. For him, Mr. Harper was here one day and gone the next. Brute doesn't know where he went or why he has not returned, which is likely the reason his behavior changed."

Brand had never thought about that before, but it did, indeed, make sense. "He has improved upon coming here, although I have never seen him quite this friendly. It gives me hope that I will be able to return him to Catherine soon. If we keep him too much longer, my mother will likely give him to the next peddler who comes along."

Miss Gifford did not laugh or smile as he'd expected. Instead, she appeared worried. Brand could only wonder at what she might be thinking.

"What is it?" he asked.

She was quick to rid the concern from her face. "Nothing at all, my lord."

Brand refused to allow her to shrink back into her shell

when they had been making such progress, so he pressed her. "Do you think my mother unkind for wanting Brute out of our stables? He is a large dog and has been the cause of much destruction in her gardens, you know."

Something akin to alarm appeared in Miss Gifford's eyes, and she quickly shook her head. "Not at all, my lord. I would never presume to think ill of your mother. She has been nothing but kind to me."

"Then what are you not saying?"

She dropped her gaze to the ground, looking decidedly uncomfortable, but Brand refused to retract his question. He wanted her to answer it. He wanted her to feel comfortable speaking her thoughts and opinions. He wanted her to cease being so blasted reticent.

When she spoke at last, her voice was so quiet he had to lean in close to make out her words. "I only worry that Brute is behaving better because he has found a replacement for Mr. Harper in you. If that is the case, the moment he is returned to Mrs. Harper will be the moment he begins to misbehave again. Only it could be worse as he will be made to suffer yet another loss."

Brand had never considered such an outcome before, but now that Miss Gifford brought it to his attention he realized it was a valid concern—one he should not dismiss, not if he really wished to help Catherine.

"In other words," he said slowly. "I may have only worsened matters by trying to help."

She shook her head again. "That is not what I meant, sir. You have definitely not worsened matters. Only look at how content Brute is here. I simply wonder if you could make the transition easier on him by asking Mrs. Harper to visit on a regular basis and spend time with her dog. She could take him on a walk about the grounds or play fetch with him—whatever it takes for Brute to feel comfortable in her presence. Perhaps then he will be more inclined to return without further incident."

Brand nodded, thinking her advice sound. Miss Prudence had been right about her sister's knack with animals after all. She had also been correct in thinking that a stroll with Miss Gifford and Brute would be just the thing. Miss Gifford had never spoken so openly or candidly with him, never smiled in quite that way, and he was certain he had never heard her laugh before. He rather liked her this way.

But would this version of Miss Gifford stay even when Brute was no longer around, or would she duck back into hiding, afraid to speak openly once again?

The fear prodded Brand into asking, "If I can convince Catherine to do as you suggest, would you be willing to join us and show her how to go about earning Brute's trust?"

The invitation didn't seem to delight her in the least. "Surely someone who knows more than I would be of more use to you, my lord. I am by no means an expert on animals."

Brand wanted to groan in frustration. He had finally landed on a plan that could help Miss Gifford feel more at ease with him, yet she hesitated. Why? It had been her idea. Did she honestly think she wouldn't be of help, or was she simply uncomfortable with the thought of spending more time with Brand?

Regardless of her reasons, he couldn't let this opportunity pass. If there ever was a chance for them to bridge the distance between them, this was it.

"I think you are mistaken, Miss Gifford," he said. "It is obvious that you know more than you think you do, and I would very much appreciate any assistance you can offer. Would you be willing to at least give it a go?"

She finally peeked up at him with fearful eyes. "What if I am wrong?"

"What if you are right?" he returned.

She bit down on her lower lip, and her fingers began fidgeting together. He had never seen her look more uncomfortable, but he did not back down.

At long last, she nodded. "I suppose I could try."

Brand felt as though he'd at last made some headway in a long-fought battle. He could not yet claim a victory by any means, but it was a step in the right direction. "Would Monday be too soon for you? If Catherine is willing, I can send my carriage for you at two o'clock."

"There is no need to send a carriage for me, my lord. I will come."

Brand cautiously took her gloved fingers in his, prodding her to lift her gaze to his. When she did so, he peered into eyes that looked a trifle lovelier than they had before. "Thank you, Miss Gifford."

She nodded, then blushed and ducked her head once more. But she didn't pull her hand away immediately, and Brand counted that as progress.

"Did my sister tell you I had an affinity for animals?" she asked quietly.

The question caught Brand off guard, and he wasn't sure how to answer. Did Miss Gifford know he had met her sister in the woods? Did she know what they'd discussed? Did she know Miss Prudence was attempting to help them? Why else would she ask such a thing unless she knew *something*?

Miss Gifford's gaze followed Brute as he sniffed about the garden, and a small smile touched her lips. "Pru told me that she has been . . . coaching you on how to further your acquaintance with me."

156

Was that all she'd said? "Yes, she has told me about some of your interests and suggested that I take you on a ride. She also thought you could be of assistance with Brute, and she was correct. Does her interference bother you?"

She shook her head. "I confess to feeling a little handled when I was first made aware of her schemes, but now I see things differently. You would think that I, the elder sister, would be wiser, but sometimes I think Prudence knows a good deal more—or at least *sees* more. I was so angry with her for feigning an ailment only moments before we were to come tonight, but . . . well, I suppose that I now understand why she did."

This news surprised Brand, and he couldn't help but inquire, "Miss Prudence had planned to come?"

"That was the agreement we had, but I don't think she ever planned to honor it. She said her stomach was troubling her and she needed to lie down, but I'm willing to wager that if we returned unannounced to Talford Hall right now, we would find her miraculously cured and playing with Scamp in the library."

Or scribbling one of her many stories down on paper, Brand thought to himself with an inward smile. Thoughts of Miss Prudence served to dampen his enthusiasm somewhat, and Brand was suddenly ready to return to the others.

"I am glad to know her illness is only a scheme." He held out his arm. "Shall we go back inside?"

Miss Gifford nodded, radiating happiness and contentment.

Brand wanted to feel the same, but while he was happy with the progress they had made, he couldn't keep his thoughts from straying in another direction. Miss Prudence may have been wise in remaining at home, but deep down, the rebellious and irresponsible part of him wished she had come.

TWELVE

PRUDENCE BLEW OUT her candle and watched the smoke rise and dissipate into the darkness, knowing she would not be able to write even one sentence tonight. Moonlight shown through the open drapes near the side of the bed, allowing her to see Scamp curled into a ball asleep near her feet. She smiled and laid her head on her pillow, watching the oddly-shaped shadows dance across her ceiling, all the while wondering about her oddly-shaped feelings.

Sophia had returned from the dinner in happier spirits than Prudence had anticipated. She had come directly to Prudence's room and imparted everything that had occurred at Radbourne Abbey. She spoke of the scrumptious meal, the kindness of Lord and Lady Bradden, and how handsome and charming Lord Knave had been. She told of her invitation to return on Monday and expressed her delight and doubt about helping Mrs. Harper with Brute.

Prudence had listened with only half an ear, not because her sister bored her, but because she found the words so very hard to hear. Of course things had gone well. If her sister had opened up, Lord Knave would certainly wish to see more of her. How could he not? Sophia was wonderful. Prudence wanted to feel the same level of excitement that radiated from her sister, but she couldn't bring herself to feel even a portion of it. Oh, Prudence had smiled, she had laughed, and she had said all that was proper. But the sad truth of the matter was that she had never felt more envious of her sister.

It was a hollow, miserable feeling.

Even now, hours later, it clung to her. She wanted to crush it into a ball and toss it from the window, but it refused to depart, causing a great deal of mischief within her heart. Prudence had thought she understood the connection between her heart and mind. They had always worked peaceably together as equals, each contributing an essential part to her thoughts and emotions. But now they were in direct conflict with each other, waging a battle over what she should want and how she should feel. What's more, she'd come to realize they were *not* equal. The desires of her heart were far more powerful. Or perhaps her mind was simply weak.

No, she told her mind. *You will not give up this fight. You will come to be sincerely happy for your sister and see Lord Knave only as he ought to be seen.*

Her heart immediately disagreed, and Prudence had the unhappy thought that she would not be getting much sleep—if any—that night. Perhaps she could use this newfound knowledge to write a story about a doctor who could extract painful feelings and memories from a person.

Now that would be a happy tale.

THE FOLLOWING MONDAY, Prudence waited until Sophia had left for Radbourne Abbey before she set out to inspect the log in the clearing. She didn't want to happen upon Lord Knave and purposefully chose a time when he would be occupied elsewhere.

Her only hope was that the rain from the previous night had not completely ruined his answers—if indeed, he had responded. Surely he had by now. As a result of her suggestion, the situation with Sophia had taken a turn for the better. Any man of honor would uphold his end of the bargain.

She picked her way slowly through the woods, thinking she should probably leave well enough alone and not seek his opinion on anything more, but how could she not? If she wished to write as genuinely and accurately as possible, she needed Lord Knave's help. That, and she couldn't deny a certain curiosity as to what his answers would be. Perhaps they would displease her and she would find it easier to dismiss him from her mind.

The hope was a fledgling one. She couldn't imagine him saying anything that would displease her.

Why did the man have to be so blasted charming? Why couldn't he be like Mr. Winston—kind and honorable, but dreadfully dull?

Not that she would wish such a person upon her sister.

Dash it all.

Prudence drew in a deep breath. The air felt heavy and moist from the night's rain, and the smell of vegetation permeated her senses. Normally a brisk walk out of doors on such a morning would clear and invigorate her mind, but today the overcast skies felt more confining than freeing. Prudence couldn't shake the sensation that she was being given a taste of what heartache felt like. She ought to be grateful for the knowledge as it would come in handy with her stories, but she didn't feel the least bit appreciative at the moment. She only felt . . . sad.

How could a person she had known for such a short amount of time consume her thoughts so thoroughly? That was the crux of the matter, really. It did not feel like a brief acquaintance. It felt as though they had grown up climbing trees and imagining various adventures together.

How was that even possible?

At least you can claim a liking for your future brother-in-law, she thought wryly.

Prudence had almost forgotten about Scamp trailing along beside her until the puppy began yipping and racing in the direction of the clearing. He was obviously anxious to meet up with their friends again.

"I'm afraid you are to be disappointed, little one. Brute and Lord Knave cannot be our friends any longer, only our acquaintances. You can blame me if you'd like. It is my fault, after all, for allowing myself to develop a tendrè for the man. But in my defense, it felt completely out of my control. It's not as though I set out to do it, you realize. It simply happened."

Scamp paid her no heed, pulling on the restraint with as much strength as his small body possessed and leaving Prudence to follow behind.

She spotted the log the moment they reached the clearing. Scamp began yipping incessantly, probably trying his best to be heard, but no large mastiff came running, and Lord Knave did not materialize before then. Prudence had known that would happen. She had planned for it. Why then, did she feel a keen disappointment?

She shook off the feeling as best she could and walked to the log, determined to get what she had come for and drag Scamp back home. But when she pulled the sodden paper from the hole, she was disheartened to see that it was only a scrap—not nearly large enough to contain the answers for even a small portion of her questions. She carefully unfolded it and had to read the words several times before she was able to decipher the blurred letters.

We did not account for England's unpredictable weather when we formed this plan. Look under the large rock at the base of the oak tree on the south side of the clearing. —K

Curious, Prudence turned around and examined the tree. Sure enough, near its trunk was a large rock sitting atop what appeared to be freshly turned dirt. She looped Scamp's restraint around a branch jutting out of the log and walked over to the tree. It took a bit of effort and muddied her gloves dreadfully, but at last she was able to slide the boulder aside. Underneath, she found a large and square tin container with a lid affixed to the top.

A thrill of excitement shot through her. She pictured herself as a pirate or explorer on the hunt for some mystical buried treasure. What could it be? she wondered as she pried open the box to reveal some folded pages of foolscap, along with a sharpened pencil and several blank pages.

She looked over the contents for a moment before unfolding the foolscap. The top page read:

I spent far too long composing answers to your many questions and could not risk the chance they'd be ruined, so I came up with the brilliant solution to hide a tin box in the ground. Have I sparked your sense of adventure? Do you now wish to write a story about pirates and buried treasure?

Her heart gave a little skip. How well he knew her already.

I have not only answered your many questions, but I have also left you a pencil and blank pages should you have any others. I hope you write a story fitting for Stephen and Catherine. Theirs was a match unlike any I have ever known.

I must also thank you for your assistance with your sister. I believe we are at last on the verge of friendship.

Your confidant,

Knave

P.S. If we are to be confidants, I think it fitting we do away with the formalities of Miss and Lord, don't you?

Prudence smiled at the valediction, allowing it to warm her heart even though he had become her confidant only by accident. But she couldn't deny that it felt good to share her secret with someone and even better when that someone had been as accepting of it as Lord Knave had been. The situation would be somewhat ideal if not for her growing attachment to him.

Prudence glanced through the remaining pages and felt a pull to settle down on the log and soak in his words. She had originally planned to return home as soon as possible, hide his responses beneath the floorboard in her room, and not read them until everyone had gone to bed. But now that she held his answers in her hands, she could not wait. With quick steps, she walked back to the log, gave Scamp a quick rub, and settled down among the memories of him.

On the page containing her questions, he had added a number in front of each one, and she found corresponding numbers on another paper, along with his answers written in a slightly untidy scrawl.

Question #1:

What qualities do you admire most in a woman?

Answer #1:

That all depends on who the woman is. Are you referring to a mother, grandmother, aunt, friend, or potential bride? Take, for example, my mother. I greatly admire the way she can manage my father without him realizing he is being managed. At the same time, I do not believe I would appreciate that quality as much in a wife, but perhaps I wouldn't notice it and would instead remain blissfully ignorant like my father.

Prudence smiled. He had known perfectly well what she had meant by her question, and he had avoided answering it completely. She could now see why he had included paper and a pencil in the container. Apparently, she must learn to be more specific with her questions. Were all his answers as vague?

Question #2:

Tell me something a woman would not usually know concerning matters of estate management.

Answer #2:

It is wiser and more lucrative to raise cows, chickens, and sheep than roaches or mice. A few of our guests might believe that Radbourne Abbey welcomes such pests from the sheer number of them we have discovered within our walls over the years, but I assure you that we are in the business of eradicating rodents and insects, not breeding them. Cows, chickens, and sheep, on the other hand, are encouraged to reproduce.

Prudence laughed out loud, not bothering to stifle the noise. If he continued in this vein, he wouldn't be at all helpful with her story, although a scene with a strategically placed mouse or roach could be quite humorous. The man was a wretch, that much was certain. But he was also amusing, and she liked that he had given her a reason to continue their correspondence albeit in such an unusual manner. It made her feel as though she hadn't lost his friendship completely.

Was that the reason he had left the pencil and paper—with the hope she would write again? Did she dare? Or would she be better off not doing so?

Her mind begged her to leave it alone while her heart yearned for the opposite. She tried to ignore both as she continued to read through the questions, laughing and smiling throughout. For all his words, he gave her very little information, and in the end, she couldn't resist the temptation to ask for further clarification. She *did* need answers, after all, and would it be so wrong to exchange a few notes with him?

Pushing her concerns aside, Prudence pulled out a clean sheet of foolscap, wrote a brief reply, and began composing a new set of questions that were more specific than the last. Before she could reconsider her actions, she folded the page, stuffed it into the box, and reburied the thing. Then she collected Scamp and spent the entire walk home explaining to her puppy that the only reason she had responded was because she needed answers. *Real* answers.

Nothing more.

THIRTEEN

THE WIND WHIPPED at Brand's face as he raced across the open meadow on the back of his horse, allowing Miss Gifford and her spirited stallion to take the lead. Her bonnet flapped in the wind behind her, and red hair flew about her head in wild disarray. She rode beautifully, and when they reached the other side, her cheeks glowed from excitement and exercise.

How different this had been from the last ride he had taken with her.

Brand grinned and attempted to tease her. "I now see how you come by your freckles."

Instead of laughing or returning his teasing, she began patting down her curls in a self-conscious manner. Brand suddenly wished he could take his words back. Why had he said that? He should know better than to draw attention to a feature that most considered unbecoming. If only she could realize that he only teased her about it because her freckles didn't bother him in the least.

It had been nearly a fortnight since that evening in the garden with Brute, and while Miss Gifford still showed signs of discomfort around him, those moments were gradually becoming fewer and further between. She smiled more often, talked with less reticence, and had taken a genuine liking to both Catherine and Brute. In fact, she seemed to prefer their company over his, or perhaps she was merely more herself with them, which was all the more reason he should think twice before teasing her again.

"Forgive me," he said quickly. "I did not mean to make you self-conscious. Believe it or not, I like your freckles."

She looked over at him, her expression doubtful. "I *don't* believe it."

Brand shrugged and squinted across the meadow. "'Tis true. I also think you ride beautifully, as does your stallion. He is a magnificent beast." Brand introduced her horse into the conversation on purpose, knowing it would give her something to talk about that would set her at ease. Whenever she spoke of animals, Miss Gifford spoke from her heart.

Sure enough, her smile returned, and she leaned forward to run her hand down her horse's mane. "Dominicus is magnificent, isn't he?"

"Dominicus," Brand mused. "That's an unusual choice for a name."

"Prudence thinks it's terribly staid, but she is wrong. It means 'holy to the Lord.' As he was born on a Sunday, what other name could I have given him? And besides, I knew straightaway that he was meant for great things. Sometimes I worry I am holding him back by keeping him with me, but I could never part with him. My father purchased him as a colt, and when Dominicus was old enough, our groom allowed me to help with his training. I will always remember those sessions with fondness, and I'm proud of the sweet and spirited stallion he has become."

"I'm certain it's because he has a sweet and spirited mistress."

Miss Gifford blushed and shifted in her sidesaddle, obviously discomfited. Lord Knave wondered how many times she had been complimented by a man before. Judging by the way she reacted to praise, he'd wager not a great deal. Perhaps he should bestow compliments on her more often to make her more accustomed to them.

"You are right to keep him," Brand continued. "Another owner may not see his strengths or understand him as you do."

That seemed like praise she knew what to do with, or at least believed. She nodded graciously. "Thank you, Lord Knave. You are kind to say as much."

He smiled, and they both lapsed into silence. She glanced around nervously, as though searching for something to inspire a new topic of conversation. Brand might have asked if she planned to comment on the blades of grass underfoot or the overcast skies above, but he didn't want to cause her further embarrassment. Perhaps she would choose to speculate on whether or not rain would shortly fall—or perhaps *he* should speculate on it.

Prudence had chastised him over this very thing not so long ago. He pictured her in the clearing, shaking her head at him in a frustrated manner. *Honestly, my lord, the weather? Could you think of nothing else to say?*

At least we have progressed to speaking about animals now, he thought, already knowing what her response would be.

Yes, but if that is the only thing you can talk about, it is not much better than the weather, is it?

"What do you find so amusing, my lord?" Miss Gifford's voice cut through his thoughts, and Brand realized he'd been carrying out a conversation in his mind. Good grief. Had it truly come to that?

He shook his head to clear his mind, then blurted out the only explanation he could think of. "I was remembering Catherine's expression the other afternoon when Brute charged at her."

Miss Gifford laughed—a rare sound from her. "It was priceless, wasn't it? I had no notion eyes could grow that large."

"I'm sure it came as quite a shock to her. Brute has only ever run to greet Stephen or me. She hadn't expected him to come barreling at her and probably thought he'd run her over."

"But he didn't."

Brand shook his head. "No, no he didn't. He's growing fond of her, isn't he?"

"Yes." She smiled, but there was a hint of concern in her expression as well. Brand could only guess at the reason, but if it was the same thing that worried him, he understood. When Brute returned home with Catherine, what would he and Miss Gifford have to discuss? What reason would she have to come to Radbourne? What goal would they share?

Brand had no answer to any of those questions. Maybe he would need to get a dog of his own—an unruly beast in need of training. His mother would love that.

"Shall we be off, my lord?" said Miss Gifford. "If I am to make myself ready for the picnic this afternoon, I should return sooner than later."

He gestured in the direction from whence they had come. "After you."

She signaled to the groom who had followed them to alert him of their plans, then spurred her stallion forward. Brand did the same, not feeling disappointed that their ride had come to an end. The sooner he returned Miss Gifford safely to her home, the sooner he could check the hidden container in the clearing.

Are you incapable of a sincere answer, my lord? Three

170

times now I have asked you the same question, trying to make myself clearer with each attempt, and still you find a way to avoid answering. My patience is wearing thin, sir, and if you do not provide me with a straight answer this time around, I shall have to take more drastic measures. Do you wish for me to call on Mrs. Harper and introduce myself? If so, continue dodging my questions, although I must admit your answers have amused me a great deal.

But really, my lord, I must know what a man of wealth and leisure might do with his mornings. Do you sip chocolate in bed? Do you peruse the newspaper? Does your valet select your clothing, or do you? Do you go for a morning ride or walk the grounds? Do you breakfast with your parents? Do you follow any sort of routine, or do you like to shuffle things around and keep life more interesting?

Your last note asked if I planned to pattern my story after Mr. Harper or you, and my answer is the same as it always has been. Mr. Harper, obviously. But since I am unable to ask him my questions, they must fall to you. So, for pity's sake, please cease your teasing and give me something I can use. It seems most unfair that your courtship of my sister continues to progress while my story does not.

Your irritated friend,
Prudence

Brand smiled, liking that she had at last signed her name without the "Miss." It had taken several exchanged letters to convince her to do it, and she had finally conceded.

After his first note, in which he'd signed "Knave," she had responded with "Miss Prudence Edith Gifford," no doubt making a point. In a postscript, she'd added, *Knave on its own has a wicked ring to it, and I could never think of you in such a way. Therefore, Lord Knave it must be.*

Brand should have let the matter drop, but he couldn't resist the challenge to convince her otherwise. He told her that true friends did not use such formality, therefore Prudence it must be. And if "Knave" sounded too wicked for her delicate ears, she could choose between one of the following: Brand, The Extraordinarily Saintly Knave, or The Devilishly Handsome Tempter of Women.

She had addressed her next letter to "Brand, the Wretch" and had signed "Miss P" to the bottom.

Brand had laughed out loud before scribbling out his reply.

> *Prudence,*
> *Pray tell, does Brand, the Wretch sound less wicked than Knave?*
> *Brand, the Wretch*

She had responded on the same slip of paper.

> *Perhaps not, but it is more fitting.*
> *–Miss P*
> *P.S. Will you kindly answer at least one of my q's? You truly are a wretch.*

After that, Brand had, at last, taken the time to answer her most recent questions, though he could not resist the temptation to not really answer them. If he gave her thorough responses, she would eventually cease needing his help and their delightful correspondence would come to an end.

As much as he should want that very thing to happen,

he could not desire it. She never accompanied her mother and sister to social events, and although he often hoped to encounter her again in the clearing, he never had. This was his only remaining link to her, and his entire being protested the thought of giving her up completely. Not yet, at least.

But he could not continue to provide her with silly answers to her questions either. As she put it, it was unfair of him.

Brand removed the pencil from the box, wandered over to the fallen log, and sat down to compose another letter. He addressed it to "Prudence," kept his teasing to a minimum, and sincerely answered one of her questions. The others would have to wait for another time.

PRUDENCE REMOVED BRAND'S latest letter from the container and settled as comfortably as she could on the log, wishing she could shake the guilt that had been her constant companion since that morning. Sophia had asked to join her on her walk, and Prudence had reluctantly agreed even though she wanted nothing more than to rush to the clearing and unearth the container. Less than ten minutes into their walk, Prudence realized that Sophia only wanted to discuss the state of things between her and Lord Knave—something Prudence couldn't bring herself to listen to. So she'd feigned a headache and returned indoors, only to sneak back out again when she spied Sophia riding away on her stallion with a groom not far behind.

She berated herself for being a dreadful sister, not that she was about to go after Sophia and offer a listening ear. In this one thing, Sophia would need to find another confidant. Prudence could not take on that role. But she could have tried harder to change the subject and speak with her sister about other things—and she *would* try harder. Another time.

For now, she intended to set aside all thoughts of her sister and read Brand's latest letter. Sophia saw him on an almost daily basis, be it while working with Brute, attending a dinner party, or galloping across the countryside. Prudence only had this one thing. Was it so wrong to keep it?

Dear Prudence,

Consider me chastised and repentant. You have exercised enough patience with me and my ridiculous answers that I will not ask you to do so any longer, though I am glad to know you found them amusing. From this point forward, I promise to do my utmost to answer at least one of your questions as sincerely and genuinely as possible in each note. Sadly, I can only respond to one today, but I will do my utmost to answer them all at some point in the near future. In the meantime, would you do me the kindness of numbering them in order of importance to you?

Your friend and confidant,

Brand, the wretch no longer

Question:

If you were to meet a woman who made an impression on you, to what extent might she occupy your thoughts in the days that follow your encounter? Would she occupy them at all?

Answer:

That all depends on the sort of impression she makes. If it is a bad impression, she might occupy my mind a little, like an irritating memory one must push from his mind every so often. If she makes an unremarkable impression, I would probably not think much of her until we met again, at which time I would remember thinking neither ill nor well of her. If she makes a good, but unexceptional impression, I would think well of her, but I would not give her much thought beyond that. If she happens to make a sensational impression, and this is a very rare thing for me, she would occupy my mind a great deal more, especially if she is a woman who should not be on my mind. That is the way of it at times, is it not? When something is forbidden to you, the allure is greater. Or is the allure greater because she is sensational? I do not know.

This time Prudence did not giggle or laugh or call him a wretch in her mind. Rather, she let the paper fall to her lap and swallowed, wiping her suddenly clammy hands across her skirts. What had he meant by that? Had he used the word "sensational" on purpose, because that was the word she had used to describe their kiss, or was it merely a coincidence? And if she *was* the forbidden woman he spoke of, was he only drawn to her because he shouldn't be?

Prudence examined her own feelings on the matter and determined the same did not hold true for her. Her feelings towards Brand had nothing at all to do with the fact that she shouldn't care for him and everything to do with the fact that she did. She liked that he made her feel things she never had before, that he listened, accepted her, and did not think it necessary to change her. And oh, how he made her laugh.

Only she was not laughing now. She was aching and feeling like the most horrible of sisters. Perhaps she should begin signing *her* name as "Prudence, the wretch."

No. She should not be signing her name at all on any letter addressed to Brand. She should not be writing to him or thinking of him or secretly wishing her sister would not find so much to like in him. Prudence had been using her story as an excuse to keep their connection going, but in reality, that had very little to do with it. She may have chastised him for not answering her questions, but she had not meant it, not really. How could she when she loved reading his replies?

This must stop.

Ever so slowly, Prudence refolded the letter and stuffed it into the pocket sewn into her shift. Without numbering the priority of her questions or responding to his note in any way, she replaced the lid on the container, set it back in the hole, and slid the rock over top.

It was time to leave Lord Knave alone and allow him to fully woo her sister.

FOURTEEN

BRAND HELPED MISS Gifford into his gig and jumped in next to her, taking the reins in his hands. Out of habit, he glanced at the upper windows of Talford Hall, hoping to catch a glimpse of Prudence. For a brief moment, he thought he spied her peeking out from one of them, but her face disappeared in an instant, leaving only a quivering curtain behind. Disappointed, Brand returned his attention to the horses, wondering why she'd stopped leaving notes and questions and chastisements. He had returned every day for nearly a fortnight, only to find the container unchanged. At first, he had assumed she'd been occupied with other things, but after several days of no response from her, he knew it was something else.

She had stayed away on purpose, and Brand missed her. If only she'd have waved or smiled or at the very least met his gaze.

She is wise to stay away, he thought, though it did nothing to cure his displeasure.

With a little more force than necessary, he whipped the reins to spur his matching grays onward. The gig lurched into motion, causing Miss Gifford to emit a squeak and slide backwards.

Brand muttered a curse under his breath before slowing

the horses down and offering a speedy apology. "Forgive me, Miss Gifford. It was not my intention to unseat you."

"It's perfectly all right, my lord." She didn't sound the least bit put out as she adjusted her skirts. "I enjoy fast-moving horses. I was simply not expecting such a speedy start is all. Your grays are quite lively, aren't they?"

More and more, Brand was coming to appreciate Miss Gifford's even-tempered personality. She didn't upset easily and had always been quick to forgive any thoughtlessness on his part. He found it easy to admire and respect her in many ways, but try as he might, he could not make himself feel anything more for her than that.

There was a time he might have been content with such feelings, but now that he'd been privy to something stronger and more enticing, he yearned for it.

"It is a remarkable day today, isn't it?" Miss Gifford had tilted her face towards the sun and closed her eyes, no doubt enjoying the warmth it offered, along with the rich scents of fall. Indeed, the day was remarkably beautiful, but her mentioning the weather yet again only reminded him of the distance between them.

Brand suddenly felt an urgent need to discuss something other than the state of the skies or animals. Surely they could connect in some other way. "Tell me, Miss Gifford, if you had an entire afternoon to spend at your leisure, how would you spend it?"

She appeared surprised by the question at first, but then her brow furrowed in thought. After a moment, a small smile lifted her lips. "That depends. Is the day as glorious as it is today?"

"It is as you decide."

"A day entirely in my power?" She grinned. "I do like the sound of that. Hmm . . ." Her gloved finger tapped

178

against her lips, reminding Brand of Prudence, only with her it would have been a pencil instead of her finger.

Devil take it. Stop thinking about her.

"Would I have control over the reactions of others—or perhaps their lack of reaction?" Miss Gifford asked.

Brand had no idea why she would ask such a thing but nodded nonetheless. "The day is yours to command."

"Then I believe I would begin with a vigorous ride on the back of Dominicus without a bonnet or gloves. I might even borrow a pair of my father's breeches and ride astride."

The ever-poised Miss Gifford wished to ride astride? Brand would love to see such a sight.

"After that, I would take a pair of scissors to the pillow I have been attempting to embroider for ages now and shred it to pieces. Then I would toss the shredded fabric into the nearest fireplace and watch it burn with delight. If, as you say, I can control the reactions of others, I would tell my mother to swallow her lecture and smile instead, and I would tell Prudence to stop laughing."

Brand chuckled, enjoying her version of an afternoon. Where had this side of Miss Gifford been hiding, and what had prompted her to throw caution to the wind this afternoon? "Pray do not stop there. What next?"

"I would drink several cups of chocolate and be sincerely tempted to pour what was left over the keys of the pianoforte. But I wouldn't actually do it as Prudence is quite gifted on the instrument and, though she'll never admit it because it would please our mother, enjoys playing on occasion."

Brand wished that Prudence's name would stop entering the conversation because it was making it difficult to forget her and focus on her sister. But he was coming to learn that the two women were close and would probably always share a portion of each other's imaginary afternoons. He could not fault Miss Gifford for that.

"I would then go for a swim in the pond behind our house." She sighed wistfully. "I do so love to swim. It is so . . . freeing, is it not?"

Brand glanced at her in surprise. She knew how to swim? He could not picture her swimming any more than he could picture her feeling stifled by her life. She seemed so well-suited to her situation. Yet here she sat, yearning for freedom and independence.

"How did you learn to swim?" he asked.

Her cheeks turned a rosy hue as though she'd unintentionally revealed something she would have preferred to keep to herself. She dropped her gaze to her lap, and her fingers nervously played with the folds of her dress. "I, er . . . our solicitor's son taught me."

Brand wondered if he'd heard correctly. "Your solicitor's *son*?"

She nodded. "When his father would come to discuss business dealings with mine, Hugh would come along. His mother had recently died, you see, and his father didn't wish to leave him home alone. He had been asked to wait below stairs, but that first meeting went on for hours and he grew tired of waiting. So he escaped out the servants' entrance and happened upon me in the gardens. He asked if I would play lawn bowls with him, and we found some empty canisters in a shed and a large rock that was not round at all. We attempted to bowl until my governess called for me. After that, whenever I knew the solicitor was coming, I would sneak away from my lessons and meet him in the gardens. We climbed trees, created imaginary worlds, built a fort, and swam—though we only dared to do the latter when his father warned him the meeting would be a lengthy one. We had the most marvelous time together."

She smiled at no one in particular, and Brand wondered if she had forgotten that he sat at her side. "He once told me that my hair was his favorite color and that I should stop wearing bonnets because they were always getting snagged in the trees or bushes." She laughed lightly. "That is one of the reasons I enjoy removing my bonnet when I am out of sight of the house. I always remember what he said to me, and I feel . . . almost beautiful."

"You *are* beautiful," said Brand.

Her eyes darted to his, and her cheeks turned bright red. "Forgive my ramblings, my lord. I don't know what came over me. You must think me absurd."

Brand began to chastise himself for not keeping the compliment to himself until he realized the ridiculousness of the thought. He had only told her the truth. She *was* beautiful, especially when she lowered her guard. What was so wrong with pointing that out? If they married, would he be made to spend his entire life guarding his tongue, even when it came to compliments? And why would he think her absurd? Did she see him only as a toplofty gentleman, incapable of understanding the joys of lawn bowls or swimming? Would they ever be able to move beyond whatever it was that wedged itself between them?

Brand led his horses off the road and stopped the gig, turning to his companion. "What happened to Hugh?"

The question seemed to quiet her anxieties. She stopped fidgeting and peered into the distance, her profile more solemn than before.

"One rainy spring afternoon, my governess caught us coming out of the woods drenched and covered in mud and laughing hysterically. He had been holding my hand to help me through some muck, and she misinterpreted the gesture for something more and immediately reported the incident to my parents. They were so angry and shocked by my behavior. I remember feeling as though I had committed a grievous sin for forming a friendship with a boy of lower birth. For years, I could not understand how something that had felt so good and joyful could have been so wrong."

Her hands flew to her cheeks, and she shook her head. "Goodness. I don't know why I am telling you this. I have never mentioned it to another soul."

"Not even Prudence?" The informal use of Prudence's name slipped out before Brand could rethink his choice of words, but Miss Gifford didn't seem to notice.

"No, not even her. I was only just out of the nursery when I met Hugh, and all of our adventures happened in the short span of a year. In a way, I was selfish with his friendship and didn't want to share him with anyone else. But more than that, I worried that if anyone learned of my secret, he would be taken from me, which is precisely what happened. After that wonderful, rainy day, my father dismissed his solicitor, and I never saw Hugh again." She looked at him with a pained smile. "We can't always hold onto the things we cherish, can we?"

Brand's thoughts went immediately to Prudence, and he shook his head. "No."

In a surprise move, she placed her hand over the top of his, giving it a light squeeze. "You're kind to listen and not think me absurd, Lord Knave. I am very grateful to you."

Her words reminded him of the way Prudence had thanked him for much the same thing. Brand had to wonder how two sisters, who were as close as Prudence and Miss Gifford seemed to be, could keep secrets from each other.

He looked down at her gloved hand on his, realizing he felt . . . nothing—no yearning to intertwine his fingers through hers, no desire to pull her to him and wrap his arms around her slim figure, and no longing to kiss her. He only wanted to comfort her, make her see that she *was* beautiful, and tell her to stop withholding herself from others.

"I would never think of you as absurd, Miss Gifford, only kind, genteel, and lovely."

She seemed to believe him this time for she slid closer, peering up at him with trusting eyes. Before Brand could say anything more, she leaned forward and pressed her lips to his. It caught him unaware, and his body stiffened. Her lips were soft and slightly cool. She held them perfectly still, as though she had never kissed a man before and didn't know how to go about it. For a moment, he attempted to return her kiss, but nothing had ever felt more wrong, so he took her gently by the shoulders and pushed her away.

She stared at him for a moment, her eyes bright with humiliation. "Forgive me. I should not have done that. I was simply overcome by your kindness, and . . . oh, my. If you did not think me ridiculous before, you must certainly think so now."

Brand continued to hold her shoulders. She felt so fragile, so breakable, as though one wrong word from him would send her skittering back into her shell, never to surface again. He wouldn't wish such a fate upon her, but he couldn't continue to force something that was so at odds with his feelings. In that kiss, she had shown him that if he continued to court her, if he asked for her hand, if he made her his wife, she would freely give what he could never return. She wanted to experience joy to its fullest. She wanted to swim, ride with abandon, surround herself with animals, and be cherished the way that young solicitor's son had cherished her friendship years before.

She *deserved* to be cherished.

Brand couldn't offer her that, and if he continued to

pretend that he could, she would come to realize that it wasn't her but her sister who held his heart. The truth of it would surely break her.

Brand had always prided himself on being a man of honor, and up until now, he thought that marrying for the sake of his family's estate was the right thing to do. But now, seeing the hurt written clearly in Miss Gifford's eyes, he realized that he had been wrong.

His father would never understand. Perhaps his mother wouldn't either. But Brand understood, and he refused to injure Miss Sophia Gifford anymore than he already had.

He took her hands in his and held them tight, desperate for her to understand as well. "You are not ridiculous, Sophia. You are intelligent, beautiful, honest, and remarkable. It is me who has been dishonest with myself and with you, and for that I must beg your forgiveness. I have come to admire and respect you a great deal, and I used to think that was enough. But it isn't—not for me *or* you. Somewhere there is a man who will make you laugh the way I have never been able to. He will make you feel comfortable and understand you in the way that I cannot. He will want to take you by the hand, not out of duty but out of love and adoration, and he will want to keep you at his side for as long as he can. That is what you deserve, and it is something I cannot give you."

Her fingers trembled in his, and her eyes shown with unshed tears, but she attempted to smile nonetheless. "You sound like Prudence."

He gave her fingers a squeeze. "Is it so wrong to have dreams? To want more than . . ." He let his voice trail off, unsure how to finish the sentence.

"More than kindness, admiration, and respect?" She shook her head. "I suppose not. I only wonder at the possibility of it." She slipped her hands from his, and her eyes blinked rapidly to contain the tears. Her voice trembled when she asked, "Will you take me home, my lord?"

She made a valiant attempt to veil her emotions, but Brand could see plainly that he'd upset her. It broke his heart, and he couldn't bring himself to return her home in such a state.

"I am truly sorry, Sophia," he said. "I wish I could offer you more, but my heart is already pledged elsewhere. I have tried to ignore it these past weeks, but I can do so no longer. It wouldn't be fair to either one of us, especially not you."

Her shimmering eyes darted to his for a moment, only to look away again. She wiped at her cheeks with her hand, and when she returned them to her lap, Brand noticed the tear stains on her gloves.

Devil take it, he thought, hating himself for allowing things to progress to this point. He hadn't wanted to hurt her, hadn't meant to do so, but it had happened nonetheless. Why hadn't he realized the futility of their courtship before now?

"Before I return you to Talford Hall," he said gently, "will you answer one question?"

She nodded, still not looking at him.

"Do you care for me in that way I described? Are you the best version of yourself around me? Do I make you laugh? Do you yearn for my touch? When I have deposited you at your door, do you await our next meeting with impatient anticipation? Am I in your thoughts constantly and relentlessly?" He held his breath, hoping she did not feel more for him than he did for her.

"That is more than one question, my lord."

Brand smiled a little, liking her show of backbone. "They require only one answer."

"I . . ." she began, her voice quivering. She stopped and cleared her throat. "Is that how you feel about the woman who holds your heart?"

Brand swallowed, wondering if she knew of whom they spoke. "Yes."

She nodded slowly, her lips pressed together. At last she spared him a glance. "I suppose my answer is no then. Perhaps I could have grown to care for you in such a way, but I am not there yet. I think I only wanted to feel that way because you were my only choice. Prudence often speaks of love and romance as though it is a requirement for a happy life, but I have never had the luxury of being able to dream as she does."

Brand tentatively touched her hand, and when she did not shrink away, he closed his fingers around hers. "Now you do. Somewhere out there is a man who will make you happy. I don't know who he will be or when you will meet him. I only know that if you dare to believe in the possibility of it, you will cross paths with him one day. I will make sure of it."

She snickered, but the sound contained no mirth. "How, exactly, will you do that, my lord? Will you conduct interviews with all of the eligible men in London this upcoming season?" She peeked at him with a sad smile.

"I might," he teased, his voice soft. In a more serious tone, he added, "I will not rest until I have made things right."

Her smile dimmed, replaced by a look of compassion. "You have already made things right, my lord. You have been honest with me and have done so in the kindest way possible. The wrong thing would have been to ask for my hand and spend the rest of your life yearning for another. I might have been content with a marriage based on mutual respect and admiration, but not at the expense of your happiness. It may not seem like it at present, but you have done us both a great service, and for that I thank you. I can only hope and pray my mother will come to see it that way."

Brand blinked, humbled by her words. She had every reason to despise him, but she didn't. She had somehow looked beyond her own disappointment and was now offering *him* comfort. She was a wonder. His respect for her increased even more, and he reaffirmed his vow to do everything in his power to help her find a man worthy of her.

"Don't worry about your mother—or father. I will speak to them both, along with my parents."

She nodded, appearing relieved by his offer. "I don't envy you that task, but I will gratefully accept your offer. I have no wish to impart such news. Perhaps if it comes from you, she will understand, though I wouldn't wager a farthing on it. Not that I am doubting your powers of persuasion. I simply know my mother to be of a stubborn, headstrong nature. She likes her plans to unfold according to her wishes."

"In that case, I shall do my best not to cower before her."

She laughed lightly. "I have no doubt that you will. Now, if you will kindly take me home and give me time to change into my riding habit and escape to the stables, you may request an audience with my parents and be done with it."

"Do not say *you* are a coward, Miss Gifford," he teased as he collected the reins.

"I readily admit that I am. And you called me Sophia earlier. I wish you would continue to do that. We can go our separate ways as friends, can we not?"

"Yes, we most certainly can, Sophia, but only because you are a woman of astonishing character. Any other woman might have tossed me from the gig and left me to my own defenses. I would not have blamed you if you had."

She smiled. "You speak as though I have done you a kindness by allowing you to remain in the gig and drive me home, but I assure you, sir, that as soon as you speak to my mother, you will not think it a kindness."

He laughed, giving the reins a light whip and directing the horses to turn them around. This time, they did not lurch, Miss Gifford did not slide backwards in her seat, and Brand did not stifle a curse. But that was the only positive change. Though tears no longer glistened in Sophia's eyes, the sadness remained. Brand despised himself for being the cause of it, but he could do nothing more to ease the pain of rejection. Only time could heal that.

FIFTEEN

PRUDENCE STEPPED OVER a log and tugged on Scamp's leash, keeping him from investigating an ant hill. Her fast-moving feet carried them both forward—not towards any certain destination, but away from Talford, Sophia, and that wretched clearing.

Prudence had stayed up most of the night, determined to make some progress on her story, and for the most part she had. Her heroine had only just lost her beloved husband, and Prudence almost felt as though she became the woman in the story. The emotions poured out of her—the longing, pain, sorrow, loneliness, and even anger. Her pencil could hardly maintain the pace.

But when the time came for the heroine to rally, the story came to an abrupt halt. Try as she might, Prudence could not make her heroine find even an ounce of strength within her. In the wee hours of the morning, it became apparent that she needed to improve her own spirits before writing another word, so she stashed her pages beneath the floorboard and dragged her weary mind and body to bed.

When she awakened a while later, it had not helped to see her sister climb into Lord Knave's gig with a radiant smile on her face, as though all was right with the world when it clearly wasn't, not for her at any rate.

Prudence despised the way she felt. She ought to be happy for Sophia. Pleased. Excited. Tickled beyond measure. Instead, the hideous feelings of jealousy and misery hovered near her like a shadow on a sunny day. Out of desperation, she had donned her walking boots and escaped to the outdoors. Scamp fought her much of the time, attempting to pull her toward the clearing and memories of afternoons spent in blissful ignorance of how Prudence would one day be made to suffer. How naïve she had been to think she could remain distant and unaffected by Brand.

No, it was Lord Knave to her now. It had to be Lord Knave.

Lord Knave.

Lord Knave.

Lord Knave.

When the memory of his kiss assaulted her, Prudence lashed out at a rock with her boot and injured her toe, muttering a few unladylike words. As she limped forward, she came to the realization that she couldn't stand by and watch Lord Knave continue to court her sister. She needed to leave. Perhaps she could pay an extended visit to her aunt in Sussex. Yes, that could be just the thing. New scenery, new faces, new conversations that didn't revolve around Lord Knave, and most importantly—distance. Oh, how she needed distance.

She could stay away until Sophia left for London and return to face the memories with only the servant to witness her misery. It was the perfect solution. The only solution. Surely her mother would think it a grand idea as well.

But it didn't feel grand. It felt lonely and cowardly and dreadful.

A horse whinnied in the distance, and Prudence looked up, surprised to see Talford through the trees up ahead. She must have circled around without realizing it, which was probably for the best. Her toe ached abominably.

She limped around the corner of the house in time to see Lord Knave disappear from sight in his gig, riding away from Talford and from her. It felt like a wretched omen of things to come. He had probably just dropped her sister off, which meant Sophia would be bursting to tell Prudence all about their drive and the kind things Lord Knave had said.

Scamp began yipping and charging in the direction of the gig, and Prudence had to pull extra hard to keep him close. If her foot didn't throb so very much, she would have dragged him back into the woods and extended their walk, if only to avoid her sister's happy glow.

"We must both stop this silliness," she told Scamp firmly. Then she drew in a deep, fortifying breath and pulled him inside, where, much to her surprise, she found the entire household in no better state than she.

A few servants bustled nervously up the stairs and through the foyer. Prudence caught the strained eye of the butler and asked, "Has something happened?"

He opened his mouth to respond, but her mother's sharp voice came from the parlor, silencing him. "Why has my tea not arrived yet? I called for it ages ago!"

A maid carrying the tea tray quickened her steps, appearing almost frightened. Prudence gave her a look of sympathy as she passed. Mother did not succumb to a fit of the temper often, but when she did, all those in the house were made to suffer. What had happened to cause such a stir?

"Ah, look. Tea," came her father's soothing voice. "Thank you, Izzy, for being so prompt. Come, my dear. Let us sit and have a drink, shall we?"

"Is that a spot on the carpet?"

"I see no spot," came her husband's reply.

"Just there, in that corner. Honestly, if that dreadful puppy has wet my rug again, I shall have it sent away at once. Why you were so insistent that Prudence needed a puppy I will never know. It has been nothing but a thorn in my side, and I will not tolerate its messes any longer!"

"I still fail to see a spot, and I think Prudence would be very sad to see Scamp leave us."

Prudence took a quiet step backwards, thinking it best to continue her walk after all. A sore toe was only a nuisance compared to the diatribe she would receive if her mother spied her now.

Unfortunately, her willful puppy had other thoughts. He began yipping and scampering towards the parlor.

"Prudence?" her mother called. "Is that you?"

Prudence glared at Scamp and whispered, "Now see what you've done." To the butler she mouthed, "Where is Sophia?"

"I believe she went for a ride, miss," came his response.

Drat, thought Prudence, not relishing the thought of facing her mother alone. How had her sister managed to escape when she could not? Life could certainly be unfair at times.

"Do not ignore me, Prudence. Come in here this instant!"

Resigned to her fate, Prudence allowed the puppy to scurry ahead of her. He ran straight to her father and attempted to jump up on his knee.

Her father's answering smile seemed more sad than amused, which was odd, but he lifted the puppy onto his lap for a good rub.

"Good afternoon, Father and Mother," said Prudence.

The strain around her mother's eyes appeared deeper

than usual. "It is anything but a good afternoon. Where have you been?"

"I took Scamp for a walk, just as I usually do. He has not wet anything in this house for weeks, Mother, and you cannot be rid of him. He is my puppy, and I will not be denied his companionship, especially when I cannot go out in society any longer."

Much to Prudence's surprise, her words seemed to take some of the zest out of her mother's temper. In fact, her shoulders drooped, and her eyes filled with regret. "I was only jesting about giving him away. I would never actually do such a thing. And . . . I think I have been wrong to keep you away from society. I have been wrong about a great many things, haven't I?" The last few words came tumbling out tremulously, and as she looked to her husband, her face crumbled. "Oh, my dear, what are we to do?" She leaned forward and placed her head in her hands as quiet sobs shook her shoulders.

Astonished, Prudence looked to her father for an explanation, but he only shook his head. Then he rose and handed Scamp back to Prudence before going to console his wife.

Prudence stared at her parents, trying to make sense of it all. Had someone died? Had an investment taken a turn for the worse? Had Sophia succumbed to another illness?

No. Sophia was out riding. That couldn't be it.

As she slowly left the parlor, no more enlightened than when she'd entered, she again caught the eye of the butler. Her unasked question was met with a shrug and a slight shake of the man's head. Apparently he didn't know anything either.

Prudence gathered her puppy close as she slowly walked up to her room. For a time, she kept a lookout for her sister, watching the stables through her window. But after a wretched night of very little sleep, her body soon grew weary, so she curled into a ball around Scamp and drifted off.

When she awoke hours later, moonlight shone through her windows. A tray containing soup and bread had been brought up at some point and now sat on a table near her bed. Prudence glanced at the clock at her bedside, surprised to see that it was already half past midnight. Scamp was nowhere to be seen, which meant Ruth had probably taken him out at some point.

Groggily, Prudence pulled the tray onto her lap, sipped the tea, and ate the tepid soup. Then she curled back into a ball and closed her eyes again, hoping the previous day and all of its strange and disappointing events would become a thing of the past.

"WHY THE DEUCE did you tell her that?" said Brand's father, gaping at his son with a look of astonishment. "Have you gone mad?"

Brand dropped his head to his hands to massage his aching temples. During his drive back from Talford Hall yesterday afternoon, he had decided to wait another day to speak with his parents. His conversation with the Giffords had not gone well, and he needed time to regroup before enduring another dreadful conversation. Unfortunately, he'd awakened with the devil of a headache.

Mr. and Mrs. Gifford had initially welcomed him with pleasure, but as soon as he told them there would be no betrothal between him and their eldest daughter, their demeanors turned cold—Mrs. Gifford's especially. She had accused Brand of playing with her daughter's emotions and discarding them without concern for what this would do to her reputation. Everyone had expected an announcement. What was everyone to think now? After years of planning, how could he walk away from their understanding and still call himself a gentleman?

Brand explained that he had never committed to marry their daughter and was under no obligation to do so—that it had only and ever been a possibility—but his words hadn't pacified Mrs. Gifford in the least. That possibility had been a certainty in her eyes—his Father's too, judging by the way he looked at Brand now. His son had strayed from what was expected, and no one liked that sort of surprise—not even his mother, though she appeared more troubled than upset.

A pain pounded through his head, feeling like a lead ball rolling from one side to the other.

"Yes, Father," said Brand dryly. "I have gone mad."

He should have waited until his head had ceased thudding to start this conversation. How many people would he disappoint before all was said and done? Would Prudence be upset with him as well? He prayed not. Although she had done her best to bring him and Sophia together, everything had changed along the way, hadn't it? Wasn't that the reason she had ceased exchanging notes with him—because she had become too attached and knew it would be wrong to continue?

"I'm glad you have realized that. Now return to Talford Hall at once and sort this out with Miss Gifford."

Brand leaned back in his chair, grimacing when another weighty pain thundered through his head. He had hoped he could count on his mother for at least a little support, but thus far she had said nothing. She merely sat beside her husband, her brow creased in worry.

"We have already sorted it all out, Father. That is what I am attempting to explain to you."

"Codswallop," he muttered. "You only think you have it sorted out, but you are wrong. What can you be thinking? In love with another woman? Hah! You are no more in love with Catherine Harper than I am."

Brand lifted his head to look at his father, immediately regretting the action when it brought on another stab of pain. His parents had assumed he had been talking about Catherine, which now that Brand thought about it, had been the logical assumption to make. Not only had he spent a great deal of time with her of late, observing the progress between her and Brute, but his parents had no notion of his communications with Prudence. No one did. Sophia had probably assumed he had been talking about Catherine as well.

What would their reactions be when the truth came to light? It would undoubtedly come as a shock to everyone, and Brand could only imagine what the aftermath would be.

Deuce take it, my head hurts.

At last his mother spoke. "I realize Catherine is a beautiful woman and you have a close connection to her, but I must agree with your father on this. I worry you are mistaking feelings of sympathy for love."

Brand hesitated correcting her. He needed to speak with Prudence before he revealed anything to anyone. If she did not care for him as he did her, there would be no need to reveal anything. It would simply be one more secret the two of them shared.

But he couldn't allow his parents to go on thinking that he was pining after Catherine either. That wouldn't be fair to her.

He closed his eyes and massaged his temples again, wishing the pain would depart. "It is not Catherine I speak of."

Silence followed this pronouncement, and Brand nearly smiled. It wasn't often he stunned his parents into silence.

"If not Catherine, then who?" came his father's brusque tone.

Brand grimaced as he leaned forward, pinching the bridge of a nose. "One of the kitchen maids, obviously. She helps cook out on occasion, and I'm vastly fond of her sweetmeats."

"What in thunderation?" boomed his father. The loudness of his voice made Brand instantly regret baiting them. He grimaced again, trying to ward off the fresh onslaught of pain.

"I believe he is only joking, dearest," said his mother in a quiet voice, no doubt sensing her son's discomfort.

"Of course he is," said his father, still far too loud for Brand's liking. "But even he must know that we are not in the mood for pranks."

"And I am not in the mood to continue this conversation," said Brand, slowly pushing himself up from the chair. "Please excuse me. I have the devil of a headache."

"Sit back down," commanded his father. "If you have declared yourself to another woman in such a reckless fashion, I must know who she is."

"I haven't declared myself to anyone, Father. I haven't even ascertained her feelings on the matter."

"You have not *ascertained her feelings?*" his father cried, his voice rising to a torturous decibel. "What nonsense is this? Surely you must know where her affections lie."

Brand pried open his eyes to meet his father's stare. "I do not."

"Then why send Miss Gifford packing? None of this makes any sense! Who is this woman you speak of?" His father was growing more irate by the moment, making

Brand think his exchange with the Giffords had been tame by comparison.

"I couldn't very well declare myself while I was courting her si—" Brand stopped abruptly and quickly amended his words. "Courting *Sophia*."

His father didn't seem to notice his slip of the tongue, but his mother's expression became shrewd. *Blast*. She had probably made the connection and was now wondering how Brand had come to know the younger Gifford daughter.

"How can you call her by her Christian name and claim to have no feelings for her?" spluttered his father.

Brand caught his mother's gaze and silently pled with her to keep her thoughts to herself.

"Sophia and I have become good friends, Father, just as Catherine and I are good friends. But I harbor no feelings stronger than friendship for either woman."

"What is so wrong with a marriage based on friendship?" cried his father. "A great many unions have been formed on less."

"If that is the case, why not marry Catherine?" said Brand, pointing out his father's hypocrisy.

"Because *she* is not heiress to Talford Hall, obviously."

Obviously. Brand inhaled deeply, attempting to calm his rising temper. He needed to remember that his father had just suffered a bitter disappointment. Years of planning and hoping and dreaming had come to naught in an instant. Of course he'd be upset. He had every right to be upset. His one and only son had let him down.

Compassion filled Brand as he looked down at his sire. The creases across his forehead and around his eyes made him look even older than usual. Brand couldn't leave without giving it one more try.

"Someday, I will find a way to expand this estate and

increase our holdings, Father, but I will not do so by wedding a woman I cannot love. I hope you can learn to accept that at some point. In the meantime, I have promised Catherine that I will attend her soirée tonight, and I mean to follow through on this promise, so if you'll excuse me, I really must do something about this blasted headache."

His father glared at him as he passed, but his mother merely nodded, saying nothing. As Brand exited the room, her calm and quiet voice reached Brand's ears.

"Tell me, my love, if I had been penniless when we met, would you still have married me?"

Brand didn't wait to hear his father's response because he already knew what it would be. His father loved his mother too much to ever say anything other than "Yes."

When Brand reached his bedchamber and laid his aching head on his pillow, he thanked the heavens for his angel mother.

PRUDENCE'S FINGERS FLEW across the keys of the pianoforte, playing a lively waltz. As much as she complained about the instrument, she enjoyed creating music, especially when her mother was away from home. The melodies soothed her soul, and if there was one thing her soul needed at present, it was soothing.

Prudence closed her eyes and envisioned herself dancing away at Almack's in the arms of a handsome man. He spun her around and around and around, making her laugh and feel beautiful, intelligent, and witty. It was a lovely dream—one Prudence had imagined often over the years. Sometimes the man would have blond, curly hair and mischievous eyes and other times he'd have a darker, more mysterious look about him. But as she tried to picture him now, the only face that appeared in her mind was Lord Knave's.

Her eyes popped open, and her fingers stilled on the keys. Why couldn't she rid her mind of that man? He pestered her thoughts throughout the day and invaded her dreams at night, and now she couldn't even imagine a dance without him.

A throat cleared from the doorway, and Prudence looked over to see the butler.

"Forgive the intrusion, Miss Prudence, but Lady Bradden has come to call."

Lady Bradden? Prudence frowned, wondering what the butler wanted her to do about it. Beyond a few exchanged greetings, she had never spoken to Lady Bradden. Surely the woman had not come to see her. "Did you inform her that my mother and sister are away from home?"

"Yes. She asked if you are receiving callers."

Me? How very odd. It was on the tip of her tongue to say that no, she was not, but . . . well, why shouldn't she receive Lady Bradden? Prudence could certainly use the distraction. From the time she'd awakened that morning, her family had made themselves scarce. Her parents had gone to meet with their man of business in town and Sophia had gone out riding. Again.

Talford was beginning to feel like a tomb. Any form of company would be a welcome change—even the mother of the man she was trying to forget. She hoped.

"Please show Lady Bradden in."

The butler bowed and left the room.

Somewhat nervous, Prudence rose from the pianoforte and clasped her fingers in front of her, watching the open doorway for signs of Lady Bradden.

The butler showed her in moments later, and Prudence was met with the friendliest of smiles. The woman wore a peach muslin gown with a matching bonnet. She looked lovely and fresh and happy.

Definitely a welcome change.

"Thank you for seeing me, Miss Prudence," she said without preamble. "Was that you playing the pianoforte so beautifully?"

"I, er . . ." Prudence glanced at the instrument. "I'm not sure I would call it beautiful, my lady, but yes, I do enjoy playing now and again. Please, have a seat."

Lady Bradden settled herself on a chair with a natural elegance that reminded Prudence of her sister.

"Would you care for some tea?" Prudence asked.

"No. I cannot stay for long."

Prudence took a seat across from her, curious as to the reason Lady Bradden had come. The woman was rather intimidating, and Prudence wished she had Scamp with her. His antics would have lightened her discomfort.

"You are probably wondering why I asked to speak with you."

The woman was certainly frank, Prudence thought, liking her already. "The thought did cross my mind, my lady, although I am glad you have come. This house has been far too quiet today."

"I had come to speak with your mother, but when the butler informed me that you were the only one at home, I thought I would take the opportunity to further our acquaintance. We are neighbors, after all. It seems a pity that I don't know you as well as I know your mother and sister."

Prudence smiled. "Yes. I never thought it fair that my sister was allowed to dine with your family while I was sentenced to the nursery, but such is life. Besides, I knew I would eventually get the chance to become better acquainted, considering our families will one day be aligned." Not that Prudence looked forward to that day. The very idea of having to stand in the background while her sister made her vows to Lord Knave made her want to vomit.

"Oh?" said Lady Bradden, her expression both surprised and intrigued.

Prudence immediately regretted her words. Perhaps it was only the Gifford family who spoke as though Lord Knave and Sophia were already betrothed. Lady Bradden was apparently much less assuming.

Prudence was quick to amend, "That is to say, *if* your son and my sister . . ." Goodness, how did one finish that sentence delicately?

Lady Bradden nodded slowly. "Yes, I suppose there is a very good chance we'll become more than neighbors one day, isn't there?"

She made it sound as though she'd only just come to that realization, which made no sense. Everyone in the entire town and surrounding villages knew of the understanding. Or was there something else—something Lady Bradden wasn't saying?

So much for Prudence thinking the woman frank.

"Tell me, my dear," Lady Bradden went on, "aside from the pianoforte, what other pastimes do you enjoy?"

The abrupt shift in conversation gave Prudence pause. It took a moment for her to adjust her thinking and decide how to answer the question. She couldn't very well say, *I enjoy speaking and exchanging notes with your son to discuss elements of the book I am writing. I also very much enjoyed kissing him and would dearly love to do it again.*

She felt a blush creep into her cheeks and frantically tried to think of something to say. "I, er . . . enjoy walking through the woods around our house." *And Radbourne's,* she thought wryly.

"Indeed?" That seemed to pique her interest. "Do you walk alone?"

"Not usually. Scamp accompanies me."

"Scamp?"

"My puppy."

"Oh." She laughed. "I should have gathered as much. Where is this Scamp now?"

"I asked one of the maids to take him out. He was yipping something terrible while I was trying to play. Either he doesn't care for sonatas or he was attempting to sing along. Regardless, I was not in the mood to tolerate the noise."

"I see," said Lady Bradden, as though she saw far more than Prudence did. "I must confess that I do not care much for animals. My son, Lord Knave—you are acquainted with him, are you not?"

"Er . . . yes. A little."

"Well, he has taken on this beast of a dog called Brute as a kindness to a friend, and I cannot like it at all. The animal has destroyed my dahlias and shredded my clematis vines. I'm certain his howl would make your puppy's singing sound lovely."

Prudence had to stop herself from blurting out that she was well acquainted with Brute's howl and couldn't agree more. "He sounds like quite the character."

"Yes. I'm surprised you have not encountered them in the woods. My son also enjoys walking the grounds and usually takes Brute with him."

"Does he?" Prudence asked a little too quickly and high-pitched. She looked down at her lap and fiddled with the folds of her skirt. "I'm certain he and Sophia will make the perfect pair. She is quite fond of animals as well. In fact, I believe she has been helping Lord Knave and Mrs. Harper with Brute, has she not?"

"Thankfully, yes. With any luck, we might actually be rid of the beast one of these days. Pray do not tell Mrs. Harper I said that."

Prudence had to smile at that. "Your secret is safe with me, my lady."

"I am glad to hear it. Now tell me, Miss Prudence, why is it that I haven't seen you out in society of late? I noticed you early on in the summer, but you all but disappeared after that. I assumed you had taken ill, but you appear in perfect health to me. Do you not enjoy socializing?"

Prudence shifted in her seat, wishing her mother or Sophia would walk through the door and put an end to their tête-à-tête. She didn't know how long she could go on thinking up creative and evasive answers to the woman's many questions.

"I will be attending Mrs. Harper's soirée this evening," she said at last with forced brightness.

"Indeed? That is happy news."

"I am glad you think so." Prudence couldn't feel nearly as pleased. Earlier that morning, when Ruth had breezed into her room to rifle through her wardrobe, explaining that her mother wanted her to attend the dinner party that evening, Prudence had felt only dread. She considered feigning another stomach ailment and crying off, but the memory of her mother's quiet sobs changed her mind. Prudence couldn't bring herself to go against her mother over such a paltry thing, not when something was so obviously amiss.

Lady Bradden stood abruptly and began pulling on her gloves. "I'm afraid I must be on my way. It was a pleasure speaking with you, my dear. I'm sure I will see you tonight.

Please tell your mother and sister that I am sorry to have missed them."

Prudence rose as well and watched Lady Bradden exit the way she had come—graceful and unexpected. She wondered at the strange exchange as she slowly sank back down. Normally, conversation came so easy for her, but with Lady Bradden it had felt forced and awkward. Prudence had even wished for Scamp's presence the way Sophia had often wished for hers.

Perhaps it was a good thing she would be attending Mrs. Harper's dinner party. As darling as Scamp could be, she missed the liveliness of crowds, the sounds of voices and music, and the flickering of candlelight. She missed talking, laughing, dancing, and feeling like her old self.

Yes, she would go to the soirée. She *needed* to go. If Lord Knave happened to be there as well, so be it. She would simply have to do her best to avoid him and pretend as though her heart was still whole and complete. Then first thing tomorrow, she would write to her aunt in Sussex and escape Talford Hall as soon as humanly possible.

Something needed to change, and Prudence was determined to do whatever it took to bring about that change.

SIXTEEN

PRUDENCE WATCHED HER sister through the looking glass while Ruth added the finishing touches to her hair. There was something different about Sophia. She didn't fuss with her gown like she usually did, she didn't fret about the color of her hair, nor did she look the least bit anxious. Instead, she appeared confident and in high spirits, as though she had finally let go of the fears she'd clung to so tightly.

Lord Knave's doing, Prudence thought, trying to be happy for her sister's sake instead of sad for her own. They seemed to have undergone a bit of a reversal. Sophia now exuded assurance and contentment while Prudence felt a newfound timidity and nervousness.

Also Lord Knave's doing.

"That rose silk looks much better on you than me," said Sophia, smiling at her sister. "I don't know what Mother was thinking when she ordered that color for me."

"She *wasn't* thinking, at least not about you. She has always assumed that if a color looks well on her it should look well on everyone."

It felt good to talk lightly with her sister again. Over the past several weeks, Prudence had pushed Sophia away, partly to protect herself and partly out of jealousy. Why she'd felt the need, she couldn't say. It's not like it had made her life better or easier. On the contrary, she had never felt more alone.

"Thank goodness I have you," said Sophia. "I would have never chosen this gold lace on my own, but it has become a favorite of mine."

"You look beautiful, Soph," said Prudence. She would have added, "Lord Knave won't be able to take his eyes off you," if the words hadn't lodged in her throat.

"Thank you." Sophia bent towards the looking glass to inspect her complexion, rotating her face from side to side. "I may have gotten a bit too brown during my ride yesterday. Do you think Mother will notice?"

"I doubt it. She's been far too self-absorbed. Haven't you noticed she's been more distressed than usual? Only yesterday I saw her sobbing about something. Do you have any idea what it could be?"

Sophia sat up straight, and a pucker appeared between her brows. She looked both concerned and even . . . guilty? She pressed her lips together and glanced at Ruth, apparently not wanting to say anything in front of their maid.

She knew something.

Prudence wanted to send Ruth from the room and demand answers, and she might have if a knock hadn't sounded on the door.

Without waiting for an answer, their mother walked in, looking both lovely and grave. "The carriage is ready," she announced in a wooden tone. Her stare was neither pleased nor critical, merely . . . vacant.

What was the matter with her?

Sophia was the first to grab her wrap. "We are ready," she said, walking past their mother with quick steps.

Prudence was slower to follow. She worriedly eyed her mother as she passed but didn't say anything.

It was a solemn group in the carriage—her parents staring aimlessly out the window and Sophia twisting her wrap nervously between her fingers. Prudence tried to inquire about the meeting in town, but her father only murmured, "It went as well as it could have under the circumstances."

Prudence wanted to blurt out, "What circumstances?" She had never felt more perplexed. What did Sophia know? Why did their parents look so grieved? Why had their mother insisted that Prudence come tonight? And why would no one enlighten her about anything?

By the time they arrived at Mrs. Harper's, Prudence felt cross with her entire family. As soon as she could, she made her escape and went in search of someone in better spirits. Even Mr. Winston would be a blessed change.

As she made her way through the throng, Prudence admired the golden walls and twinkling chandeliers. Card tables had been set up in the far corner with a few games already in progress. Along the back wall, doors opened onto an extensive balcony, allowing fresh air to spill inside. With the bouquets of flowers that had been artistically placed around the room, the ballroom felt almost garden-like. Musicians warmed up their instruments not far from where Prudence stood, and people milled about, talking and laughing.

She *had* missed this.

"Pru!"

Prudence spun around to clasp hands with her friend, as though it had been ages since they had spoken. It *felt* like ages.

"How stunning you look, Abby," said Prudence, admiring her friend's peach silk dress and white lace gloves. Abby's father might be absent much of the time, but he saw to it that his daughter was always outfitted in the latest fashions.

"Compliments will not serve, my friend," said Abby playfully. "I am very cross that you have not come to see me, especially after you promised you would."

"Do not be cross with me," said Prudence. "I have been unforgivably preoccupied, I know, but do not say I've been a disappointment. I couldn't bear it."

"Bear it you must, for you *have* been a disappointment, but not an unforgivable one. I could never be truly cross with you."

"Bless you for that," said Prudence with a smile.

"And don't you look fetching yourself," added Abby. "Is that a new gown?"

Prudence peered down at the rose silk dress she wore. "It is one of Sophia's castoffs. She gave it to me the moment she held it up and realized the rose clashed abominably with her hair. I had forgotten about it until Ruth pulled it from the back of the wardrobe earlier today. Do you really like it?"

"It suits you perfectly, as does that gorgeous knot in your hair." Abby's grin turned sly. "One might think there is a certain someone you are trying to impress this evening. Is there?"

The comment did not sit well with Prudence. She had, indeed, taken extra care with her ensemble tonight, but it was not for Lord Knave's benefit. It was for her own. At least that's what she had tried to tell herself.

"If you must know," she said. "I am hoping to impress Mr. Winston."

Abby laughed. "If that is your aim, it would have been more effective to string a necklace made of wheat about your neck than those pearls, which are lovely, by the way."

"Thank you. And you are correct, as always. Wheat would have complimented the rose beautifully."

Abby laughed again. "I have missed you, Pru."

"And I you. Now tell me, how is your steward's nephew? I'm afraid I cannot recall his name."

Abby blushed rosily, and her eyes darted around the room. She clasped Prudence's arm and pulled her away from the crowd and prying ears. "I simply must tell someone, and you are the obvious choice. William kissed me. Only once, and it was quite harmless, but I enjoyed it."

Abby probably expected Prudence to be shocked, or perhaps even appalled by this news, but she was neither. Instead she felt a camaraderie with her friend—on most counts, at least.

"Is a kiss ever harmless?" she murmured, remembering a certain kiss had harmed her a great deal.

Abby frowned. "He knows that I am bound for London next season, and by the time I return, he will have found a position elsewhere. The kiss was nothing more than a distraction for both of us."

Prudence eyed her friend, wondering if her heart was really as unattached as she claimed. "Do you care for him at all?"

The question gave Abby pause. She pressed her lips together and looked away for a moment or two before answering. "I do care for him. He is kind, amusing, and has taught me a bit about estate management, which I find interesting. He is also so attentive to me, which is not a luxury I have been accustomed to at Chillhorne. I'm very grateful for his friendship, and I did enjoy his kiss, but . . . well, I cannot explain it exactly. Only that he does not set my heart to pounding. I am comfortable with him, nothing more. Perhaps it is your influence on me, but I should very much like to meet a man who makes my heart pound."

Prudence nodded slowly, thinking of her views on romance and how silly they now seemed. She had experienced firsthand that pounding heart and felt the disappointment of it keenly. "Comfortable" sounded heavenly and far less hurtful.

"I hope you find what you seek, Abby. I really do." Silently, she added, *And I hope it is not accompanied by the pain I now feel.*

"We will both find it. I'm certain of it," pronounced Abby with a careless grin. There was a happy glow surrounding her, and Prudence felt a pang of envy. She missed grinning and laughing and looking forward to the day for no reason in particular. Lately, a somberness had settled over her, weighing her down and making her feel . . . well, *not* happy. Not precisely unhappy either, merely devoid of emotion.

Prudence didn't care for the feeling at all and would give anything to shake it free, but it wrapped around her like a cocoon, sealing her inside.

"Is something the matter?" Abby asked, peering at her friend with an expression of worry.

"Not exactly." Prudence forced her lips into a smile. "I simply feel unused to socializing and am not as comfortable in a crowd as I once was."

"That will never do," said Abby, taking her by the elbow. "I believe what we need is the Calloway twins. Have you seen them?"

"No." Prudence scanned the room for their familiar faces, only to stop cold when she spied Lord Knave across the way. Dressed in dark colors, he looked as handsome and wonderful as ever. He smiled and laughed at something Mrs. Harper said before lifting his gaze to hers.

Prudence's breath caught, her heart lurched painfully, and all she could think was, *I should not have come. Heaven help me, I should not have come.*

She quickly averted her eyes when a cotillion was announced, and her search for one of the twins turned desperate. *Will someone please ask me to dance?* At this point she'd take anyone, even Freddy, who would probably trod on her slippers.

As though reading her mind, Mr. Winston suddenly materialized at her side, bowing low over her hand. "Miss Prudence, will you do me the honor?"

"I would love to," she said quickly, her eyes darting across the room to where Lord Knave still conversed with Mrs. Harper. She sucked in a deep breath, trying to calm her racing pulse. Abby's hand was claimed as well, and the two friends took their places on the dance floor. Only then did Prudence spot one of the twins. She caught his gaze, sent a silent plea his way, and drew a small measure of relief from his answering grin and nod.

She tried her best to forget about Lord Knave as she danced with Mr. Winston, but it was a difficult feat to accomplish. As soon as Mr. Winston began telling her about the recent birth of a lamb, her mind strayed to Lord Knave. Did he plan to request a dance from her at some point? She would say no, obviously. She had to. Holding his hand, looking into his eyes, and walking through the steps of a dance with him would be her undoing.

Goodness, she needed to stop thinking about him.

She closed her eyes briefly, picturing herself as the haggard wife of Mr. Winston, toiling in the fields, milking cows, and weaving necklaces from the stalks of wheat.

Would it ever come to that?

No. Prudence would become a governess first.

As soon as the dance ended, she gratefully accepted Mr. Calloway's invitation for the next set. With him, she found it much easier to push thoughts of Lord Knave and haggard wives aside, and by the conclusion of the second dance, she felt much more composed. Her heartbeat had returned to its usual rhythm, and her face no longer felt overly warm.

"I enjoyed myself immensely, Lionel."

"You mean Felix."

She swatted his arm playfully. "Do stop teasing me, sir. You cannot claim to be Lionel one moment and Felix the next."

"But I *am* Felix."

"How can that be when it was Lionel who asked me to dance? Never say you lied to me, sir, or I shall be irritated in the extreme."

He grinned. "In that case, I am most definitely Lionel."

"You are a scoundrel as well," she said with a laugh. "Now be a dear and ask Miss Stevenson to dance. She never seems to have much fun at these gatherings, and if anyone can cheer her up, it is you."

"Your wish is my command." He didn't look too thrilled at the prospect, but he bowed nonetheless. Prudence had requested the same favor from Mr. Winston earlier and was happy to see that he'd complied as well. She may not know Miss Stevenson well, but the poor girl often looked so forlorn, standing apart from everyone else, that Prudence was determined to see her enjoy herself for once. If it took begging all of her partners to do the gallant thing, so be it.

Lionel left Prudence with her mother before going in search of Miss Stevenson. Her mother didn't look much happier than she had before, but at least she didn't chide her younger daughter for laughing or smiling or drawing too much attention. That was a nice change.

After a moment or two of uncomfortable silence, Prudence spied Abby across the way, looking a good deal happier, so she muttered a quick goodbye to her mother and began making her way towards her friend.

A waltz was announced, and several gasps sounded throughout the room. Even Prudence couldn't stifle her surprise—or amusement. She and Sophia had attempted to dance it together one rainy afternoon, but they'd exaggerated the movements in a dramatic fashion, giggling the entire time, and hadn't learned much of anything. Prudence had to commend Mrs. Harper for being daring enough to add it to the program as it would be fun to see others dancing it.

Someday, she really must meet that woman.

"Will you do me the honor of this dance, Miss Prudence?" said an all-too familiar voice at her side. In an instant, her pulse became erratic and her breathing shallow. Why did he have to come to her now? Things had been going so well.

She stared straight ahead, not daring to look at him. She had rehearsed this moment so many times in her head and thought she'd been ready with her response, but she could not remember what that was now.

Dash it all.

"Are you ignoring me on purpose?" She could hear the smile in his voice, and her heart galloped at the sound of it. How she had missed seeing that smile.

Ever so slowly, she turned to face him, trying with all her might to keep the anxiety from her expression. She shook her head and whispered. "I cannot."

"You cannot ignore me or you cannot dance with me?"

"Both," she squeaked, her eyes pleading with him to leave her be.

"Why not?" he asked, pretending as though he didn't already know the answer.

"I . . ." She grasped for the first excuse that came to mind. "I don't know how to waltz."

He grinned, and her stomach gave a little flip. "You're

in luck then. I have danced it numerous times and would be glad to instruct you on the steps. There are only five of them, you know. It's not difficult to learn, I assure you."

"I cannot," she repeated, imploring him not to make a bigger scene than he already had. From the corner of her eye, she could see her mother staring at them disapprovingly, along with several others.

"Of course you can." He took her by the hand and guided her onto the dance floor. Not wishing to make a scene, Prudence followed, trying with all her might to come up with a way to extricate herself from the situation. He should be asking Sophia for this dance, not her. What was he about? And where were the Calloway twins when she needed them most?

Prudence gasped as Lord Knave rested his hand at her waist and pulled her close. He felt warm and strong and wonderful and smelled like a mixture of sandalwood and citrus. Any willpower she had left began to crumble like a dried piece of cake.

"You start with your feet together like so and move first to the right—my left—and around in a box-like pattern. Follow my lead," he whispered in her ear, sending chills down her spine. It took several spins for Prudence to gather her wits about her and learn the rhythm of the movements, and at last she stopped tripping over his feet.

"I knew you would catch on quickly," he said with a smile.

She glanced around, grateful to see they were not the only couple on the floor. Lionel had followed through on his promise to ask Miss Stevenson to dance, and Abby tried not to wince when Freddy trod on her toes. Even Sophia was there, stumbling through the steps with Felix.

"Why did you ask me to dance and not my sister?" Prudence breathed.

"I have already danced the second set with your sister, and it would be rude of me not to ask you as well."

"You should have danced the waltz with her," she hissed, feeling some of her spark return.

"Why would I do that when I wished to dance it with you?" The way he looked at her caused her heart to spin so fast she suddenly felt dizzy.

"You have been avoiding me," he continued. "Why?"

She glared up at him, despising him for making her say it aloud. "You are to marry my sister, sir."

He had no reaction to this. He merely continued to spin her around the room. "Do you *want* me to marry your sister?"

"I . . ." Prudence floundered. She *should* say yes. It was the right thing to say, the right thing to want. But it wouldn't be honest, and while she stretched the truth at times, she couldn't make herself lie outright. "I want you to do whatever will make you and your parents happy."

"What if the thing my parents desire is in contradiction to what *I* desire?" he asked. "What would you have me do then?"

She peered into his beautiful blue eyes and felt herself become lost to them. Goodness, he smelled good. Prudence ached for him to hold her closer still so that she might rest her head against his chest. The room spun around her, blurring like a painting that had been left out in the rain.

"What is it you want?" she whispered, almost afraid of his answer.

"You."

She missed a step and stepped on one of his boots. She would have stopped dancing if his strong arms hadn't continued to carry her along. Her heart pranced and her mind whirled as her feet tried to maintain the pace.

He desires me.

The thought thrilled her like no other had ever done. It lightened and lifted and twirled her around until another thought tossed her back down.

I've stolen my sister's intended.

Merciful heavens, what have I done?

Music thudded in her ears, sounding more like the clamoring of hooves than a talented orchestra. Voices and laughter and the clinking of crystal only added to the chaos. Prudence had dreamed of a moment like this, she had wanted it so very badly, but not in this way. How could she welcome happiness while her sister faced rejection?

She couldn't. It wouldn't be right.

Why was Brand telling her this now, in the middle of a crowded room where they had already garnered a great deal of attention by dancing the waltz? What was she to think or do or say? How was she to feel?

Her body began to tremble at the onslaught of emotions, and tears stung her eyes.

You will not cry. You will not!

"Do you care for me?" he asked.

She wanted to fib and say that no, she didn't. She wanted him to return her to the outskirts of the room, where she could escape to the privacy of an antechamber and compose herself. She wanted him to stop making this all so wretchedly hard.

"I do care for you," she finally admitted. "But that doesn't mean I should."

"Why shouldn't you?"

"Please, Brand, I'm begging you," she whispered, her emotions on the brink of erupting.

He tightened his hold on her, and as they whirled past the doors leading to the balcony, he pulled her outside. The world still spun, and Prudence might have lost her balance had he not tucked her arm in the crook of his elbow and held her close. A few people milled about, but Brand paid them no mind as he led her to a shadowed corner, away from prying eyes and ears.

It wasn't until a breeze whipped around her that Prudence realized how warm she had been in the ballroom. The cool air felt wonderful and served to calm the pounding in her head.

Brand turned her to face him, taking both of her hands in his. "You have obviously not heard."

"Heard what?"

"Sophia and I have agreed that we will not suit. We do not care for each other the way we should—the way I care for you."

She gaped at him. He and Sophia were not to marry? When did this happen? How did she not know? Why hadn't Sophia or her parents said anything? Did her mother and father even know?

Suddenly, it all made sense. Her mother's quiet sobs, her father's grim expression, the heaviness that had hung over Talford Hall like a cloud of disappointment. They knew. They all knew. Even Lady Bradden had known.

But . . . Prudence frowned as she thought of Sophia— the lightness in her eyes, her cheerful disposition, her newfound confidence. Had that only been an act—a way to mask her pain?

It had to be.

"Say something," Brand whispered.

Prudence shook her head. There were too many words, too many feelings. How could she possibly know what to say? It felt as though she'd been standing unprotected in a meadow when the skies let loose torrents of rain. Shame . . .

Joy . . . Dread . . . Wonder . . . The emotions were all there, pouring down on her in sheets and making her wonder if she might drown in them.

"Lord Knave, unhand my daughter this instant."

Jolted from her thoughts, Prudence looked to see her mother standing before them, trembling with barely controlled anger. She stared at Brand with cold, hard eyes, daring him to defy her. Sophia stood a step behind, looking confused and stricken.

Prudence wanted to shrink into the shadows and cower from everyone and everything. This was all her doing. Her need to spy on Brand that morning from the tree, arrange to meet him in the clearing, pester him with questions, and beg him to kiss her.

Her unwillingness to let him go before it was too late.

Brand slowly released her hands and took a step back, keeping his eyes on her. He seemed to be imploring her to do something, but for the life of her, she couldn't understand what.

"Sophia, please ask your father to summon our carriage."

Prudence flinched at the sound of her mother's voice, but it wasn't until she caught the gleam of unshed tears in her sister's eyes that she felt the throb of them. It pierced deep inside her, creating a hole that might never mend.

A crowd of people began to cluster around them, witnessing the horrible scene. Prudence took in the familiar faces before looking back to Brand, silently pleading with him to say or do something to right the wrong she felt in her heart.

He didn't. He merely offered her a curt bow and a look of remorse. "I shall call on you tomorrow, Miss Prudence."

"You will do no such thing," hissed her mother.

Brand's jaw tightened as he directed a steely gaze at the woman. "I shall call on you as well, Mrs. Gifford. We have much to discuss. Good evening to you."

His eyes lingered on Prudence for a moment longer before he strode away, taking all the warmth with him. As soon as he disappeared into the throng, Prudence felt the chill in the air. She wrapped her arms around herself and caught Abby's saddened gaze.

A great gulf seemed to open between her and those around her, swallowing up their good opinions. Even Abby and the Calloway twins stood on the other side.

How had this happened?

You have too many secrets.

Prudence had once read that everyone ought to be allowed a secret or two. It had sounded so harmless and perhaps even wise, but she didn't think so any longer. When secrets created a wall between people, as they had done with her and her sister and her friends, they most definitely should *not* be allowed.

PRUDENCE WOULDN'T HAVE believed it possible, but the drive home from the soirée was far more somber than the ride there. Sophia trained her gaze out the window, not sparing her sister even a glance, and her mother had a stony set to her jaw. Her father appeared neither pleased nor displeased, merely thoughtful in a worried sort of way. No one uttered a word.

Prudence loathed the silence. She wanted to fill it with explanations, apologies—*something*—but the words evaded her. They sat jumbled in her head, no more sorted by the end of the ride than the beginning.

Sophia went straight to her room, leaving Prudence to face her parents alone. They ushered her into the study and closed the door while she stood in the shadows, head held high as she awaited the accusations.

"How could you?" whispered her mother. Her words contained no bite, only disappointment, which surprised Prudence. She had expected a severe scolding.

"I did not mean for it to happen, Mother. I—"

"You don't understand. You never have." Her mother dropped down on the sofa in a gesture of defeat. "You have been blessed with everything—beauty, talents, a vivacious personality, and a kind heart. I have always known that men would be drawn to you over your sister. I wanted to keep you at home for another year, but your father convinced me it would not be fair. Your sister's illness was not your doing, and you should not be punished because of it. But that did not keep me from worrying."

Prudence stood as still as she could, but her body trembled from the weight of it all. Her mother had told her of this concern before, but Prudence hadn't paid it much heed. She had thought it silly and unwarranted, but not anymore.

"There is something else you do not know," her father said, sounding weary. He approached the fireplace and stared down at the remnants of a burnt log on the grate.

"Years ago, we made the mistake of replacing our solicitor after a . . . worrisome occurrence. Unbeknownst to us, our new solicitor began falsifying numbers and stealing from the estate. When everything came to light, he disappeared, taking the bulk of our capital with him. We would have lost everything if not for the kindness of your Uncle James. He enabled us to remain at Talford, but only just. The effects of our solicitor's deceit still hangs over us and probably always will. We have never told you or Sophia of this because we didn't want our worries to become yours, but the truth of the matter is that we have next to nothing. Your sister is heiress to a barely surviving estate, and you will inherit nothing. We cannot provide you with even the smallest of dowries."

"We had it all planned out," inserted her mother. "Sophia would marry Viscount Knave, they would see to it that you had a London season, and you would make a successful match as well. I have never worried about you as I have Sophia. She does not have your looks or talents, and although our family is respectable, we claim no exalted connections. Her inheritance is all she has to offer, and what gentleman would consider Talford Hall, in its current state of debt, an inducement?

"Do you understand now, my dear girl? Lord Knave was your sister's one chance to make a successful match. I know London society, and I know she will not take, especially without a proper dowry. If Lord Knave intends to marry you in her stead, only think of the additional damage that will do to your sister. Should you marry first, you will be sealing Sophia's fate as a spinster. Under any other circumstance, we would be thrilled that you have secured the affections of such an eligible man, but how can we when it comes at the expense of your sister?"

Prudence could remain standing no longer. Her legs gave way, and she sank down on a nearby chair. Yes, she understood now. Not only had she stolen Lord Knave but she'd taken away her sister's chance for happiness.

Was that really the case? Had Prudence ruined everything? Was there no hope at all for Sophia? No. She refused to believe it. She had more faith in her sister than that.

"We do not tell you these things to injure you, my dear," said her father. "You say you did not mean for this to happen, and we know that is true. You do not have a malicious bone in your body. We simply wanted you to understand why we cannot be happy by this evening's turn of events."

Prudence nodded, thinking of Brand. She pictured him standing before her in the clearing, his eyes crinkling at the edges when he smiled and his lips quirking as he tried not to laugh. He had accepted her without judgment, helped her with her stories, and became her confidant and her friend. No. He had become more than that. A mere friend would not cause her heart to soar at the sight of him or turn her world topsy turvy with a kiss.

She adored him. She cherished him. She loved him.

That was the tragedy.

Love shouldn't feel like this. It should be thrilling and exciting and magical—and it had been for a few precious moments. Prudence had felt all those wondrous emotions. But with that wonder came shame and guilt and the realization that love did not treat people fairly. It embraced some and forgot others, and where was the wonder in that?

With a heavy heart, Prudence pushed herself to her feet, glad that at least one secret had surfaced this evening even though it had been a heartbreaking one. Now that she understood her family's situation better, Prudence saw her mother in a different, kinder light. Instead of the strict, controlling woman Prudence had always thought her to be, she'd become . . . a mother. A person who cared and worried and wanted what was best for *both* of her daughters.

Prudence swallowed against the raw lump in her throat. "I am so sorry. Please know that if there is something I can do to set things to rights, I will do it. I did not mean for any of this to happen."

"We know, my dear," said her father. "We know."

Prudence could stand it no longer. She turned and fled the room, not stopping until she had reached her bedchamber. Once there, she paused on the threshold, drew in a shuddering breath, blinked back her tears, and held herself together long enough to be helped into her nightclothes. Only after Ruth left did Prudence crawl into bed, gather Scamp to her, and finally let the tears come.

SEVENTEEN

AS SOON AS the sun began to glow through the clouds on the horizon, Prudence collected her half-written story from the box beneath her floorboards and walked across the hallway to her sister's bedchamber. The room was dark and quiet, and at first Prudence thought her sister was still asleep, but Sophia lifted her head to glance at her sister, only to drop it back down with a thud.

"I hope you slept better than I did," Sophia muttered, stifling a yawn.

At least she was speaking now. Prudence went to the windows and pulled the coverings aside, letting the early morning light invade the room. Sophia groaned and rolled to her side, but she didn't insist her sister close them again.

"I didn't sleep a wink either," said Prudence as she climbed onto the bed and tucked her legs beneath her, fingering the stack of foolscap on her lap.

Sophia opened one eye and frowned at the pages. "What are those?"

Before she could lose her nerve, Prudence pushed the unfinished manuscript towards her sister. "I don't just like to read novels, I like to write them. Someday, I hope to be a novelist."

Sophia slowly lifted her head, looking at the pages in surprise, her long, red braid falling forward.

"I first encountered Lord Knave near his hunting lodge when I went to spy on him the morning after the Hilliard's ball. I overheard him make an assignation with Mrs. Harper, and I wanted to investigate, thinking I would uncover enough proof to convince you that he was not worthy of you. I was also curious about what they might say or do. All I knew about romance came from books, and I wanted to witness something real. What I saw, however, was a meeting between two friends for the sole purpose of putting another friend and husband's memory to rest. There was nothing remotely romantic—or nefarious—about their assignation. In fact, I came away feeling as though he might be worthy of you after all."

Prudence continued her story, leaving nothing out. She told Sophia how he had learned about her scribblings, how she had offered to help him with her sister if he would help her with her story. She told Sophia about the kiss she had practically begged him for, about their agreement not to meet in the woods any longer, about the buried box and what she had thought was a harmless exchange of notes.

"Only it wasn't harmless. I eventually realized that and determined I would never return. I planned to write Aunt Madeline this very morning, asking if I could come for an extended visit."

Prudence swallowed, hoping her sister wouldn't despise her forever. "I never set out to get in the way of his attachment to you, but I managed to do exactly that. I am so dreadfully sorry, Soph. I am sorry I did not tell you about my scribblings. I am sorry I didn't give you a full account of our encounters in the woods. I am sorry I convinced myself that I was doing you a service when it was a monumental disservice. I am sorry for everything."

Sophia had no answer to this. She merely propped her head up with her hand and picked up the first page of Prudence's story. Only after she had skimmed through it did she look at her sister. "You're a writer?"

"Not really. At least not yet," said Prudence. "I only want to be one."

"Does Mother know?"

"Heavens no."

"Father?"

Prudence shook her head.

"Abby?"

"No."

"Only Lord Knave?"

"And you."

"Why did you not tell me before?"

Prudence drew her knees to her chest and pulled her nightdress around her ankles. "I was afraid that if you knew, you would think less of me. How silly that concern seems now. I would rather you think me imprudent than a cold-hearted thief."

Sophia set the pages aside and considered her sister. After a few moments, she spoke. "I will confess to feeling betrayed by you last night, but that was the only reason for my sorrow—that and the disappointment I caused Mother and Father. Lord Knave was right to walk away from our arrangement. Although we became friends, I never could be myself when I was with him. We were trying to make something work that was not meant to work, and it always felt like . . . well, work really.

"Yesterday, when I went out riding, I realized something. For the first time in years, a wonderful feeling of liberation surrounded me. I know Mother and Father worry that I will never marry, and maybe I won't, but I am no longer afraid of that outcome. I would rather become a spinster than marry someone who made me feel trapped the rest of my life. Don't you see, Pru? You have not stolen anything from me. On the contrary, you have set me free. You have opened the door for me to seek my own happiness, whatever that may be. How could I possibly think less of you for that?"

Tears welled in Prudence's eyes, and she leaned forward to throw her arms around her sister. "I don't deserve you."

"Marry him, Pru, if that is your wish," whispered her sister. "I will be all right."

An overwhelming feeling surged through Prudence, teaching her about the power of forgiveness and love and selflessness. Not only did it mend past hurts and mis-understandings, but it forged a bond between her and her sister unlike anything Prudence had ever felt. They had always been close, but now nothing stood between them. They were sisters in every sense of the word.

Sophia pulled away, wiping away tears of her own. She sniffed and pointed to the stack of papers. "Can I read this?"

"It's not finished," said Prudence. Perhaps it never would be.

"I don't care about that. And who knows, maybe I can be of assistance?" It was a question—one that brought to mind Brand's earlier words.

Why not make her your confidant?

Why not indeed?

Prudence should have done so long before now. The day she had used what little pin money she had to purchase some pencils and paper instead of ribbon and lace was the day she should have trusted her sister with her innermost desires. Sophia might have laughed. She might have thought her sister mad. But perhaps she would have also offered to read her scribblings as she had just done.

All this time, a quest that had felt like a lonely endeavor could have been shared. They could have sneaked into each other's bedchambers in the dead of night and talked and laughed and giggled over possible scenes and adventures and outcomes.

Yes, secrets did erect walls. Perhaps in some instances those walls were good, even necessary, but when it came to her and Sophia, they'd been nothing more than a barrier. How much Prudence had missed over the years. How much they both had.

"I would love your help, Soph."

Sophia grinned and crossed her legs, pulling a pillow onto her lap. She leaned forward and rested her elbows on the pillow and her chin in her palms. "Since we are revealing our secrets this morning, I suppose there is something I should tell you."

Prudence's eyes widened in a look of feigned shock. "You have a secret? No, I don't believe it. You're far too proper, poised, and above reproach for that."

"Do you wish to know it or not?" Sophia teased.

"Yes, please." Prudence scooted to the head of the bed and wrapped her arms around her knees, watching her sister expectantly. "I'm listening."

"Well, since you are so fond of stories, you are sure to like this secret, although it is a mite tragic," said her sister. "It's a tale about a younger version of me, a young solicitor's son, and a friendship that was doomed from the beginning."

PRUDENCE STROLLED DOWN the stairs just as her parents emerged from the back hallway. She inhaled deeply and squared her shoulders, preparing to face somber count- enances. Last evening, she had promised she would do something to correct all the commotion she had caused, and after a great deal of reflection, she had formed a plan. It wasn't foolproof by any means, or necessarily a great one, but it was a plan.

The only plan.

She would explain that they needn't worry about their daughters. Sophia would still have her season in London, and even without a dowry, she would catch the eye of someone worthy of her. Prudence was sure of it. If it took two or even three seasons, so be it. Prudence would discover some way to pay for them—perhaps out of the proceeds of her first published book. Was that too hopeful to contemplate? Probably, but it felt better to hope than to doubt.

In the meantime, Prudence would remain unattached at Talford Hall, at least until Sophia married. Then, and only then, would she allow herself to consider a future with Brand, assuming he was still amenable to the idea.

It could work. No, it *would* work.

Prudence reached the bottom of the stairs and faced her parents. "Mother, Father, I wish to speak with you." Much to her confusion, they appeared calm, content, even hopeful. It caught Prudence off guard, and she found herself scrambling to remember what it was she wanted to tell them.

"Good morning, Prudence," said her mother good naturedly, nodding as though nothing was amiss.

"Er . . . good morning." Prudence looked from one to the other in confusion. "Is everything all right?"

"Quite," said her mother. "In fact, your timing couldn't be more fortuitous. We were about to send for you."

"Indeed?" There were moments when Prudence believed she had sorted through every possible outcome, leaving no room for surprises, only to find herself very surprised. This was one of those moments. Had her parents formed a plan of their own? Did it include washing their hands of their younger daughter?

Prudence wouldn't blame them if it did.

"You look frightened, my dear," said her father with a humorous glint in his eye. "Rest assured, we don't intend to send you to the gallows just yet. We only wanted you to know that you have a visitor waiting to speak with you in the study."

"A visitor? At this hour? In the study?" Prudence blinked, trying to wrap her head around everything. She had never received anyone in the study. That had only ever been her father's domain, especially at this time of the morning. What on earth was going on? Were her parents tipsy? Had it come to that?

No, they appeared too alert for that.

Could it be Brand in the study? Had he followed through on his promise to call on them? Surely not. A visit from him would not please her parents in the least. Only last night her mother had told him not to come. She wouldn't be the least bit happy if he defied her wishes.

But what other explanation was there? Perhaps Mr. Winston had come to offer sound farming advice in exchange for their younger daughter's hand in marriage.

Her father seemed to find her bewilderment humorous. His eyes twinkled merrily. "Off you go now, child. Do not keep him waiting."

Prudence cast a wary glance at her parents as she walked past them, but they didn't move to follow. Instead, her mother took her father's arm, and they began strolling up the stairs in perfect harmony with each other, as though it was an everyday occurrence to allow one's daughter to meet a man alone in the study.

Prudence paused in front of the partially closed door

and peered inside the darkened room. Although the window coverings had been pushed aside, the cloud-coated skies dimmed the sunlight, giving the room an eerie feel.

She pushed open the door quietly and stepped inside, her breath catching when she spied Brand standing before the far window, looking out at the dreary morning. Her heart lurched, and she took a moment to admire his broad shoulders, straight back, and confident stance. He looked splendid in his buff-colored buckskins and blue jacket. She wanted to rush to him, wrap her arms around his waist, and feel his warmth and strength. She wanted him to hold her close, tell her everything would be all right, and curl her toes with another kiss.

Prudence forced her feet to remain still as she tried to keep her turbulent emotions from her voice. "It's rather early for a morning call, my lord. I haven't even breakfasted properly."

He turned and smiled, his eyes soaking her in. "How is it you are already dressed and looking as lovely as always. I had expected to wait at least an hour."

"An hour?" she said in mock astonishment. "Do you think me so in need of primping as that?"

"No. But when an unexpected caller arrives at an unseemly hour, well, not even a man could ready himself as quickly as you did."

Prudence clasped her hands and shrugged. "I *am* quite talented."

"Agreed." He chuckled, moving in her direction.

Prudence sidestepped behind the sofa, placing her hands on the spine as she watched him approach. "Speaking of talents, I must know how you managed to turn my parents up sweet. Last night they were curmudgeons, and this morning they appear to be happier than I have seen them in years. I cannot understand the transformation. What magical gift do you possess, sir?"

"Only the gift of reason." Brand began to walk around the sofa, but when Prudence moved in the opposite direction, keeping the furniture between them, he stopped and folded his arms, watching her with a devilish gleam in his eyes.

"I was thinking a Christmas wedding would be just the thing."

She tried to show no reaction to this, though her heart raced madly. "For whom?"

"Us, of course."

"Then it sounds . . . cold," said Prudence, thinking more about the effect it would have on her sister than the actual temperature.

Brand laughed. "If I promise to see to it that you stay toasty warm, will that sway you?"

"That is not what I was referring to, my lord," she said. "I could never marry before my sister. It would be cold-hearted of me. Surely my parents did not agree to such a thing."

"Actually, they were very amenable to the idea."

Prudence's mouth dropped open. She did not believe it, not after everything they had told her last night. Brand began walking towards her once more, and Prudence again moved away.

"Will you please stop doing that?" he asked.

"No."

"Why?"

"Because if I allow you any closer, I will feel more addled than I already do, and I must make sense of everything first. Did you cast some sort of spell on my parents? And what of Sophia? Do you not care at all for her well-being?"

"I am not a wizard, and I care a great deal for Sophia's well-being."

"Then how can you even contemplate a wedding so soon?"

"Because I believe it will be in your sister's best interests. And mine." He grinned.

Prudence blinked at him, attempting to understand how that could possibly be true. It couldn't, could it? She frowned. "For pity's sake, my lord, will you please cease this silly game and speak plainly? I did not sleep a wink last night and don't have the patience for this."

He quirked an eyebrow. "Are you always this cantankerous in the morning?"

"*Sir.*"

He laughed. "Very well, I shall tell you. But only if you cease moving away from me and let me hold your hands."

It seemed a fair agreement, so Prudence nodded, allowing him to approach and take her hands in his. He had discarded his gloves at some point, and his hands felt warm and smooth and wonderful. He threaded his fingers through hers and ran his thumb across her palm. Delightful shivers shot up her arm.

"That wasn't so difficult, was it?"

She swallowed, thinking herself a ninny for letting him touch her.

"If we marry in December," he began, "Sophia will be the subject of talk and speculation. Some gossips might even put her on the shelf, even though she is not yet twenty. There will be no avoiding that. But I do not believe such talk will last for long, not when she will make her bows as the sister of The Viscountess Knave.

"We will all go to London together—my parents, your parents, Sophia, and the two of us. We will reside in our

236

townhouse on Grosvenor Street and attend only the most esteemed social events. I will be sure to put it about that it was your sister who put an end to our understanding. Those conditions, combined with her handsome dowry, will hopefully make her one of the more sought-after debutantes."

Prudence took a moment to consider his words, thinking it all sounded quite perfect with the exception of one thing. "Didn't my parents tell you? Sophia has no dowry. We are destitute, my lord. This estate is all we have. From what I understand, Sophia's inheritance isn't much of an inheritance any longer."

He brought her hands to his chest and pulled her close enough to smell the sandalwood and citrus scents that always lingered about him. "You did not let me finish," he murmured.

She looked up at his handsome face and waited as patiently as she could for him to continue.

"Years ago, my father offered a large sum to purchase the northwesternmost thirty acres of Talford Hall's property. Your father refused but suggested they encourage a match between the heir of Radbourne and heiress of Talford instead. Father agreed, and everything seemed to be going according to plan until I had the indecency to fall in love with the younger Gifford daughter. As you have already pointed out, my actions, coupled with your father's debts, placed your family in a difficult position."

"Yes," said Prudence. "Will you please tell me something I do not already know?"

"My, you are impatient," he teased, kissing her fingers.

"Something else I already know," she pointed out, making him chuckle once more.

"When I realized the full extent of your family's difficulties, along with my contribution to them, I made an offer to your father. In exchange for your hand in marriage and the same thirty acres my father has desired for so long, our family will pay off your father's debts and provide him with enough capital to begin anew and provide his eldest daughter with a sizable dowry. Yes, it will mean a loss for Talford Hall, but it should not affect the value too greatly. It is only unused land my family desires, not the tenant farms."

At last, Prudence began to understand. Her parents' about-face, a December wedding, Sophia's brightened prospects. She shook her head, not yet daring to hope. Could it be that simple? She looked into the eyes of the man who had come into her life so unexpectedly, turned it upside down, and now offered to right it beautifully.

Yes, it could be that simple.

Prudence couldn't resist the temptation any longer. She threw her arms around his waist and hugged him tightly, burrowing as closely as she could. "Your father has agreed to all of this?"

"Not yet, but he will."

She pulled back enough to peer up at him. "How can you be certain? The land couldn't possibly be worth as much as you have offered for it."

"The land is worth a fair amount to my father, but you are correct in thinking he will balk at the price. My mother, on the other hand, will not, and she will convince him I am right. I'm not sure how she will do it, but she will. As I mentioned in one of my notes, she's rather adept at managing my father."

Prudence smiled, feeling light and giddy and so very happy. "That sounds like a useful skill. Do you think she would be willing to instruct me on how she goes about it?"

He framed her face with his hands. "You already know how it's done, my love. Simply ask me anything, and I will do it."

Prudence's heart warmed, crackling and popping like a cheery fire in the grate. She dimpled. "Will you continue to answer any and all questions I have regarding my stories?"

"Yes."

"Will you introduce me to Mrs. Harper so that I might ask *her* some questions?"

"Yes."

"Will you kiss me anytime I wish?"

"Most definitely."

She combed her fingers through the hair at the nape of his neck and eyed him coyly. "Must I tell you when I wish it, or will you just . . . know?"

He chuckled and pulled her tightly against him, murmuring, "I'll know," before kissing her with a passion she couldn't have imagined on her own. Her world became alight with color and magic, whirling her about in a beautiful waltz. Brand could deny being a wizard all he wanted, but Prudence knew better. He had waved his wand, placated her parents, formed an ingenious plan, and offered her a life she had only been able to dream about before.

He had made the impossible possible.

When at last he drew back, he cradled her face in his hands. "Do you intend to write our story someday?"

She shook her head, still reeling from the kiss. "I don't think so. I want it to be ours and ours alone."

He smiled, searching her face. "Have I told you how much I adore you?"

"Only adore?" she teased. "How can that be when I am madly in love with you?"

"Are you mad enough to marry me in the chilly month of December?"

"You did promise to keep me warm."

"And so I shall, my love, so I shall." He proceeded to give her a small taste of that warmth.

EPILOGUE

THE CHURCH BELLS rang loudly as Prudence floated from the church on the arm of her husband. Despite the bite in the air and the dreary skies, she felt wonderful. Under her white, fur-lined pelisse, she lifted her lace skirts to descend the steps and smiled at all those lining the path, waiting to wish them well.

She kissed her mother and father on their cheeks, clasped hands with Lord and Lady Bradden, and hugged her sister and Abby tightly. Several smiles and well-wishes later, the couple climbed into the coach and waved from the window until it lurched forward into a slow and steady pace that would eventually deposit them at Radbourne Abbey for their wedding breakfast.

Prudence turned from the window and tilted her head up, wrapping her fingers around Brand's neck. "Hello, my husband," she said as she pulled his mouth to hers. He kissed her quite thoroughly, wrinkling her gown and loosening several strands of her hair, before wrapping an arm around her and tucking her against his side.

"Are you warm enough?" he murmured, placing another kiss on her temple.

"I should hope so," she said, rearranging the lace around her knees. "Several bricks have been placed at our feet, there are more on the seat across from us, and another at my side."

"I did promise to keep you warm."

She laughed and rested her head blissfully against his shoulder. "I should have known you would exceed all my expectations. You always do."

"And I plan to continue to do it for at least a lifetime."

She sighed happily, wondering again how she had been fortunate enough to earn the love of such a man. Not so long ago, her dream to fall deeply in love had felt so elusive and out of reach, like trying to catch a hummingbird within the palm of her hand. But somehow, she had captured that dream and watched it unfold into a beautiful reality.

Her mother had once warned Prudence not to expect a dashing man to spirit her away, but that was precisely what Brand had done. Perhaps not in the way she'd always envisioned, falling madly in love with her on first glance and romancing her until she agreed to marry him, but he *had* done it. He'd swept her into an adventure unlike any other, filled with joys and sorrows, thrills and disappointments, hopes and doubts—an adventure Prudence had no control over, much as she'd wanted it at times. But that was the beauty of a real story versus an imagined one. Prudence had learned that it was the uncertainties in life that gave it color, complexity, and depth.

She wouldn't have it any other way.

"Is something amiss?" Brand asked, running his fingers along her cheek. "You seem pensive all of a sudden."

"I'm grateful." She placed a kiss on his hand and relaxed against him. "And perhaps a bit tired as well."

His eyes sparkled with amusement. "Do not say you were up scribbling away and burning the midnight oil on the eve of our wedding."

"I had to," she explained. "I promised Sophia I would finish the story before we left on our wedding trip, and I had but one scene left to write. She has been dying to read it in its entirety, and I felt the pressure to comply."

Brand shifted positions to look her in the eye. "It's done?"

"Yes. Last night—or rather, early this morning."

"And you're only now telling me this?"

She blinked at him, somewhat surprised by his interest. She had assumed he'd grown tired of listening to her prattle on about scenes and characters and plots.

"Did you want me to bring it to your attention during our wedding ceremony?" she asked with a smile.

"No, but—please do not say you have given it to Sophia."

"I did."

He stared at her, his mouth agape. "Over your husband?"

Prudence would have laughed if not for the genuine disappointment she saw in his expression. She felt a twinge of guilt because of it, but mostly, it thrilled her to know that he wished to read her story.

"You were not my husband this morning," she pointed out.

"No. I was your *betrothed*."

"Perhaps. But you did not beg as Sophia did."

"I didn't think I would have to beg."

"But you must," said Prudence. "How else am I to know you would like to read it? Sophia made her wishes quite plain, whereas you did not."

He shook his head, turning his attention to the window, and muttered, "Incredible."

Prudence might have felt another prickling of guilt if

she hadn't been so delighted by his reaction. He was adorable when he appeared put out. She leaned into him, running her fingers between his neck and neckcloth, a touch she knew he could not resist.

"Did you really expect me to hand over my story on our wedding day?" she asked. "What would you have done with it, I wonder? Taken it with us on our wedding trip? Surely you must know I would never tolerate such a thing. For the next fortnight, you are to be mine and mine alone."

That seemed to placate him, for he chuckled and pulled her onto his lap. "Very well. I will forgive you this once. But from this point forward, you must promise that you will give any and all future stories to your husband first and your sister second."

"Agreed." She pressed a kiss to his lips, showing him precisely how much she liked his proposal. He was not a man who craved the written word as she did. On the few occasions they'd retreated to the library to read together, he preferred books on science or farming or medicine. He had never once reached for a novel.

But here he was, showing he loved her enough to read her silly stories of love, friendship, and romance. What's more, he wanted to read them *first*. She kissed him again for good measure.

The coach slowed to a stop, and Radbourne Abbey appeared in the window. Prudence sighed in protest, wanting to go on kissing her husband and keeping him all to herself.

"Shall we go in?" Brand asked softly.

"In truth, I'd rather not. But I know we must." She slid off his lap and attempted to repin the escaped strands of her hair. "How do I look?"

"As though you've been ravished." He grinned, attempting to help with the pins. His large hands were probably

244

making it worse, so she pushed them aside as the door to the coach opened.

"One moment," she called to the coachman, tucking in the last few strands. "Is that better?" she asked Brand.

"Now you look ravish*ing*. If we do not leave the coach this instant, I will not be responsible for my actions."

She grabbed him by the lapels and said, "You, my lord, are a wretch."

"Yes, but I am *your* wretch."

"Indeed you are." She smiled and kissed him one last time before he assisted her from the coach. As they walked slowly up the stairs, Brand leaned in close and lowered his voice. "How would you feel if I were to introduce Nathan and Phillip to Abby and Sophia before we depart."

She slowed her steps and raised an inquiring brow. "Your old school chums?"

He nodded. "Nathan is an incorrigible flirt and Phillip a little too passionate about politics, but they have been good friends to me and will remain at Radbourne for at least a week. They will also be in London for the season."

Prudence turned to face him, smiling coyly. "Are you attempting to play matchmaker, my lord?"

"I would never presume to take on such a role. But I do have many friends, and I plan to introduce Sophia to the lot of them during our stay in London. She may choose whom she wishes. I only desire to give her ample opportunities to find someone who will make her as happy as you have made me. If Abby should find a suitable match as well, so much the better."

Prudence could have hugged him for his answer. Up until now, she had thought she and her mother would be alone in their quest to find Sophia a worthy husband. But as she peered into the determined expression of her husband, she knew better. He was not just her husband. He was her hero—her friend, her helpmeet, her companion, and her confidant. He was someone who would read her scribblings, make sure her parents did not fall into financial ruin, and see to it that her sister married well. He would love and cherish her as he had only just vowed to do because he was the sort of man who kept his promises.

Prudence loved that about him. She loved a great many things about him. But mostly she loved that he would be hers and hers alone. Always.

DEAR READER,

Thanks so much for reading! I hope this story gave you a break from the daily grind and rejuvenated you in some way. This is the start of a new regency series with two more books forthcoming, so if you'd like to be notified when Abby and Sophia's stories are available, you can sign up for my New Release Newsletter at RachaelReneeAnderson.com or follow me on Amazon.

If you can spare a few minutes, I'd be incredibly grateful for a review from you on Goodreads or Amazon. Even though I can't thank you personally, I am always so thankful whenever readers take a few minutes to review a book.

May your days be filled with beauty and happiness!

Rachael

COMING NEXT IN THE SERENDIPITY SERIES

My Brother's Bride
The Solicitor's Son

ACKNOWLEDGMENTS

Where do I begin?

A huge thank you to my mother, Linda Marks, and my sister, Letha Wendel, for brainstorming with me, listening to my ramblings, and helping me to plot out my stories. You have both been a huge blessing in all aspects of my life.

My friend and walking buddy, Alison Blackburn, thank you for talking books with me and for being an awesome beta reader. Your perspective has been invaluable, and your insights made this story so much better.

Andrea Pearson, so grateful for you! Thank you for always exchanging manuscripts with me, for picking up or pointing out things I missed or didn't think about, and for always giving me such great critiques. You're the best!

Karey White, bless you for only being a phone call or text message away, for helping me come up with this series title, and for sharing your brilliant editing skills with me. I don't even want to contemplate what I'd do without you.

Kathy Habel, I can't tell you how grateful I am for your friendship and willingness to help me with everything from beta reading to marketing to so many other random things. You are always on top of everything, and I feel incredibly blessed to know you.

Helen Taylor, actress and narrator extraordinaire, thank you for bringing this book to life in a way no one else could. You are amazing.

My husband, Jeff, a hundred million thanks for being the husband, father, supporter, confidant, and friend that you are. You are my hero, and I love you.

Lastly, I must my Heavenly Father, for challenging, inspiring, and blessing me.

ABOUT RACHAEL ANDERSON

RACHAEL ANDERSON is a *USA Today* bestselling author and mother of four crazy but awesome kids. Over the years she's gotten pretty good at breaking up fights or at least sending guilty parties to their rooms. She can't sing, doesn't dance, and despises tragedies, but she recently figured out how yeast works and can now make homemade bread, which she is really good at eating. You can read more about her and her books online at RachaelReneeAnderson.com.

Made in the USA
Middletown, DE
12 May 2018